Job's Wife

A Novel

JEAN SHAW

Wolgemuth & Hyatt, Publishers, Inc.
Brentwood, Tennessee

The mission of Wolgemuth & Hyatt, Publishers, Inc., is to publish and distribute books that lead individuals toward:

- A personal faith in the one true God: Father, Son, and Holy Spirit;

- A lifestyle of practical discipleship; and

- A worldview that is consistent with the historic, Christian faith.

Moreover, the company endeavors to accomplish this mission at a reasonable profit and in a manner which glorifies God and serves His Kingdom.

Unless otherwise noted, all Scripture quotations are from the Holy Bible, New International Version. © 1973, 1978, 1984 International Bible Society. Used by permission of Zondervan Bible Publishers.

Wolgemuth & Hyatt, Publishers, Inc.
1749 Mallory Lane, Suite 110, Brentwood, Tennessee 37027.

Library of Congress Cataloging-in-Publication Data
Shaw, Jean.
    Job's wife : a novel / Jean Shaw. — 1st ed.
       p. cm.
    ISBN 0-943497-96-5
    1. Job (Biblical figure)— Fiction. I. Title.
PS3569.H3825J64 1990
813'54—dc20   90-30193
                                                                CIP

For Andrew, Peter, Carol, and Julia

It is not only the old who are wise,
nor only the aged who understand what is right.
(Job 32:9)

Chapter 1

I t is spring, and the irises are blooming. Against the sandstone cliffs their purple clumps look like amethyst gems in a crown of pale yellow gold. I once wore a necklace of amethysts. Job received it from a caravan traveling from Arabia. The men were near death from their trek across the desert and Job offered them lodging. I knew he would. When I saw that long, scraggly line of camels in the distance, I ordered the servants to kill a sheep. Preparation for a meal was well under way when Job came running to find me.

"Visitors are coming!" he cried. "We must see that they are cared for!"

"Calm down," I told him. "Everything will be ready. Water has been drawn and clean mats rolled out on the ground. There will be a feast to delight their swollen eyes and fill their shrunken stomachs."

In they came, smelling like rotten meat. The servant girls gasped for breath. Job, of course, pretended not to notice. He greeted each one, clasping their hands to bid them welcome. They were treated as if they were royal sheiks when it was really Job who was the great chief—a king among his troops. Seven thousand sheep he had, five hundred yoke of oxen, and five hundred donkeys. His three thousand camels made those traders' beasts look puny indeed!

Job was a generous man, always reaching out to help the poor and needy. "God's intimate friendship has blessed my house," he would say. "Therefore I rescue those who cry for help." So it was that we had a steady stream of outcasts passing through our kitchens. There was more than one victim we snatched from the teeth of death.

The traders from Arabia turned out to be unwashed gems themselves. Once they were clean and fed, they told us of their profitable trip. Their bags were full of treasures, one of which was the amethyst necklace which they presented to Job in appreciation for his hospitality. Now it was my turn to gasp as Job slipped it over my head. The stone was of the finest cut, set in a pendant of gold filigree. Job had visited a gold mine once, and he told me later that this ore was the purest possible.

I gave that necklace away after the children were killed. Just handed it to a perfect stranger! What does a necklace matter when death strikes? Can amethysts and gold bring loved ones back? I would never wear fine robes again. There would be no reason for me to make merry. My dress was sackcloth and ashes. Hardly the attire for jewels and filigree!

That all happened a long time ago. Now it is spring again, the time for purple irises. I rejoice in the warmth of this morning. Was winter more savage than usual, or do my bones and marrow take less to the cold?

How like the seasons has been my life with Job! Together we savored the sunshine of God's favor. Ten children He gave us, seven sons and three daughters. (I loved the girls but was thankful there were only three.) Job loved them all the same, taught them to love each other, and taught them to love God. He used to say that when his children were around him he could sense the presence of the Almighty. It did seem that God was very close as we sat around the evening fire, listening to Job talk about God as his dearest friend.

When our children came of age, Job gave each of them a house. To so endow the girls was almost scandalous. "Why not?" he would say. "The Lord has given me more wealth than I can ever use." I would wonder at the wisdom of making young women so independent, and he would say, "If they are independent like their mother, as sensible and quick thinking (and he would bite my ear), I will have done them a favor." Now, what could I say to that?

Looking back, not knowing how short their lives would be, I'm glad we loved our children as we did. Death can come so quickly, so very quickly! What matters then that food was spilt or bedrolls left awry because there were mountain goats to see? One morning, when the sun was half an eye peeking over the horizon, Job bundled everyone outside to see a string of the agile creatures picking their way along the ridge. "Who guides their feet?" one child asked. "Where are the babies born?" asked another. Always Job would answer, "God. God knows. God does. God cares." Always God.

When loved ones die, we sift the events of their lives through our memories, letting fall the dross and retaining the pure ore to examine time and time again. Are we not surprised at what we keep and what we throw away? When I think about the children, the gold is knowing that they loved the Lord, for what could be more precious than the knowledge that each one belonged to Him, that even today they are where He is?

What is the dross? The dross is my impatience, my anger sometimes, when my children lingered at a point of wonder. An ostrich egg, warm in the sand. The scent of a cedar tree. A hawk, spreading its wings toward the south. "Hurry up!" I would say. "We cannot stop now!" A moment when we could have been in touch with God was missed.

God forgave me, that I know, and honored what I did that was right in His eyes. Imperfect mother that I am, He took the good and blessed it. Praise His name!

Chapter 2

W hen I think about our family, our *first* family, I
think of harmony. It was remarkable how well
we got along, twelve of us with so many servants and
so many possessions. Wealth like that can tear a family
apart. I've seen it happen: arrogance, jealousy, cruelty.
Do not the Ancients tell of murder at the very beginning of things?

Daily, Job with all our household went before the
Lord. Prostrate on the ground before the altar, we would
acknowledge our sins and seek God's forgiveness. Job
would expound on the greatness of God, His profound
wisdom and vast power. He reminded us that God controls everything in the heavens. He could speak to the
sun and it would not shine! "God can shake the earth,"
Job said, and we remembered the earthquake that had
toppled the posts at the city gates, not to mention the
pottery in our own kitchen! The wails of our head cook
could be heard across the desert!

When our sons moved into their own homes, they
took turns holding feasts. They would invite their three

5

sisters to eat and drink with them. This was certainly not common among our people! Siblings were rarely so close, nor did they wish to perpetuate childhood customs.

Each day one son would host the others, and when the cycle of seven feasts had gone round, Job sent for them to come and be purified. Not that they had done something evil, you understand. "Perhaps my children have sinned and cursed God in their hearts," he said. In the midst of all that social enjoyment might there not be a momentary turning away of their hearts from God? Might they feel that enjoyment was better than religion?

So it was, every seventh day Job sacrificed a burnt offering for each of them. Ten rams would be slaughtered and laid upon the altar, Job acting as father and family priest. I can picture him standing there with his eyes lifted toward heaven, the dead animal in his hands. Its blood would be splattered on his robe. I think there is a cleansing quality in blood, don't you? I know that it is good for a wound to bleed. Blood is part of birthing, I can tell you! A woman is happy once the womb is clean. I believe that when God sees the blood spilt on the altar, He forgives our sins and makes us spotless in His sight. The Ancient Ones tell us this is so.

How the Lord blessed us in those days! Our land stretched out as far as the eye could see. A thousand oxen were required to cultivate the fields. Yoked in pairs, the animals plodded steadily back and forth, pulling the wooden plows through the earth that had been softened by the rain. They were followed by the sowers, rhythmically casting the wheat and millet along the furrows. Then came the cold days when we wore our thickest clothes. "The seeds are wearing their coats too," I told the children. "They will sleep until the earth is warmed by the spring sun."

One day they all came running in from a visit to the fields. "The seeds are awake!" they cried. "Come and see!" Pulling me out the door, we gathered at the crest of the ridge where we could see the fields extending like a pale green blanket for miles in every direction. On the hillsides grazed the sheep, guarded by the shepherds and their dogs.

Everywhere we looked, we saw God's blessing. "The hand of the Lord has done this," I reminded the children. "In His hand is the life of every creature and the breath of all mankind." We bowed our heads and thanked the Lord.

Chapter 3

For a man in middle age, Job's energy was incredible. With so much property to manage and so many servants to oversee, he still had time to take his seat in the public square of the city. The other officers were older men than he, but when Job arrived, they rose to their feet out of respect for his benevolence and righteousness. It was not my place to be present at such meetings, but Job told me how the young men stepped aside to let him pass.

If the chief men were talking, they would cover their mouths with their hands. The voices of the nobles were hushed and their tongues stuck to the roofs of their mouths, so great a man was my husband! If there was a problem to discuss, men listened to Job expectantly, waiting in silence for his counsel. After he spoke, they had no more to say. It was as if they were waiting for showers, and Job's words were spring rain to drink.

Job took his position as chief of the city council with great solemnity, but he was not overbearing. He was the kindest of men, with a warm smile that lit up his face. To young and old, the radiance of his face was precious. They knew the way he chose for them was right.

You may think Job's wealth earned him such honor. Not so! It was his concern for others that made the difference. It was said of him that he was eyes to the blind and feet to the lame. "Father to the needy," he was called once at a testimonial dinner. Job used the opportunity to encourage the other men to reach out to those who were crying for help. He felt it was his duty to take up the case of the stranger or any other victim of unfortunate circumstances.

One day Job received word of a sheep owner in the city who was dying from a fall down the mountainside. Job stopped what he was doing and hurried to the man's home. He found him lying on a mat, blood oozing from a deep gash in his head. It was obvious he could not live long. Job saw the anguish in his face, the anxiety in his eyes. "What can I do to help?" he asked.

The sheep owner spoke in a barely audible whisper: "My wife and children . . . who will take care of them? My mother was not blessed with other sons. I have no brothers to take in a widow."

Job immediately assured him that he would take responsibility for the family, even to paying one of his overseers to look after the sheep. The man's wife, kneeling by his side with wet cloths to wipe his brow, wept in gratitude. Her husband reached out to clasp

Job's hand. "May the Lord bless you with a long life and many sons," he said. Job felt the throb of life depart from the man's fingers, even as he spoke.

To Job, such acts of kindness were only expressions of his faith in God. To him there was no contradiction between theology and practice. God had given to him and so he gave to others. I gladly supported him in his benevolence, for I, too, was grateful for all that God had done. I had moments of pride, however, when I felt very good about myself. Behind the scenes, of course, I was usually the one who oversaw the distribution of food, the resettlement of the orphans. I did not think it unseemly to accept a little praise.

Of course, neither of us foresaw any interruption in the flow of God's blessings. Why would we? We were not sinning in any deliberate way. Job regularly worshiped the Lord, bringing his sacrifices to the altar. He often said to me, "I will die in my own house, right here with you beside me." He compared the number of his days to grains of sand in the desert. "That would be a very old man!" I observed, laughing. "I do not think I will be happy, married to a desert!"

To me, everything that was life was Job. Vigor, strength, growth, maturity, fruitfulness — that was Job not to mention, a great love for all of God's creation, an unending joy in its wonders. There was within Job a well of vitality that had no bottom. I pictured him as a great tree that reached down to the water deep below

the earth's surface. His arms were mighty branches
that stretched out to catch the evening dew.

Job could work from dawn to dark and still find
the energy to wrap those arms around me. We never
tired of making love, never. Some nights we would
take our mats out under the stars, our bodies burning
even in the cool night air. I did not equal Job in righteousness, but in passion he had met his match. Our
children began as seeds of love, sown in warm, moist
soil that ached for their planting.

We are, of all the people in the city, most singular
in our relationship. Job has had no other wives, while
other men have two or three. The council scribe has
five! It was said that even the Ancient Ones divided
their amorous attentions between two or more wives.
As for concubines, thank God I was spared those tro-
phies of tribal wars! They are no end of trouble, with
their foreign tongues and pagan religions. A concubine
is nothing more than a convenient relief for the pain
between a man's legs. Not that I hold them account-
able. After all, they are slaves, to be commanded at
will. Job never believed in owning slaves, male or fe-
male. We have servants who are well paid and treated
as valuable members of our household.

I have always trusted Job. He has never violated
that trust, even though he could do so in our culture
and no one would care. He told me once he even made
a covenant with his eyes not to look lustfully at a girl.
Since we each came of age we have only known each

other, a singular situation, as I said. God's law calls us to be faithful, so we keep the law because we honor God. Is it not a mystery, that in honoring God He has given us a love so bathed in fidelity?

It was my belief that I loved Job, the inner man. In reality, of course, the physical embodiment of Job's spirit was essential to my affections, although I did not, could not, know it while our lives were so full of blessing. Whom, or what, did I really love? The torturous answer to that question would reveal the true character of myself, of Job, and of God.

Chapter 4

I do not think people today take Satan seriously. To the Ancient Ones he was terribly real, the craftiest of all the wild animals, slithering about in the Garden of Eden with no other objective than to deceive Eve and Adam. Surely, they felt his power!

It is hard to convince men and women today that Satan is so *busy*. They seem to think he is some sort of slug, laboriously making his way into places where he can cause trouble. Actually, Satan roams through the earth, going back and forth, rushing here and there trying to find ways to frustrate God and destroy mankind. By his very name he is the "Accuser," a being hostile to anything that is in the best interests of God's highest created order.

I confess I did not think much about Satan until Job and I so directly felt the force of his hand. We had lived for such a long time without the presence of un-mitigated evil that I had forgotten how quickly and ruthlessly the Accuser works.

The day began as usual, with our household and the sun rising simultaneously. In the gray, cool dawn the smoke of cook fires could be seen in silvery wisps all along the ridge. We ate our usual meal of barley bread, dates, and milk. Job led us in praise to the Lord who had provided it, and we went about our tasks.

Our oldest son was planning a feast for his brothers and sisters, so the girls were doing what all girls do: deciding what to wear. I could hear them chattering away, asking the servants to bring this scarf and that necklace. Pots of eye paint were brought out, with much discussion as to its application. The girls rouged each other's cheeks, a custom they began when the eldest one became twelve and entered womanhood. That is a difficult passage in life, don't you agree? The body changes so!

The social implications of twelve are overwhelming. Marriage, children, running a household. I had been their teacher and model, a frightening responsibility for me! I could *tell* them many things, but it was what I *did* that made the real impact. Their black eyes observed my every gesture. Their sharp hearing caught the slightest inflection of my voice. I might appear cheerful as I executed my tasks, but they knew when I was irritated with the cook or exasperated with Job. Yes, there were times when their father sorely tried my patience. Patience was *his* noteworthy quality, not mine!

Our daughters knew their father would pick good husbands for them. Of course, he could offer a dowry

that was unsurpassable. What young man would reject
an offer from the wealthiest man in the whole countryside? But Job wanted more for his daughters than a
husband who could manage money. He insisted upon
finding for them partners who loved the Lord and worshiped him daily. It is faith which determines character, and Job knew that if a husband's faith in God is
strong, he will develop the sensitivity that makes a
good husband.

So, our daughters were still unmarried. There was
plenty of time, but they were older than many married
women in the city. They did not seem to mind, as they
spent so much time with their brothers. I do believe
there was in each girl an underlying trust in God and
in Job.

By noon the ritual of beautifying face and body
was complete. Accompanied by their servants, our
lovely daughters went off to the feast. The mist had
lifted, revealing a perfect winter day. Our farmers were
plowing the fields, holding the plowing sticks steady as
the plodding oxen dragged them across the earth. I remember commenting to my maid about the large number of donkeys grazing in the nearby fields.

I fully intended to go about my tasks, when I was
taken with a sudden chill. I walked back to the sleeping quarters to get a robe. As I was stretching out my
arm to slip it on, something inexplicable, sinister, unlike anything I had ever known, filled the room with
its presence. I experienced an immediate fear of suffo-

cation. My heart was beating so loudly, I wondered why a servant didn't come running to see what was making all that noise. I wanted to cry out, but my throat was full of sand.

I wanted to find Job. I needed the comfort of his arms around me, the soothing balm of his voice. Had I been able to lift my feet, I would have run to his side, but I was like a tree, rooted deep in the earth.

Does a woman have a special sense of premonition? Because women are so intimate with life, are we more closely related to death? When Job and I lost our child — the one stillborn — I had a feeling from the very first that something was wrong. That pregnancy was no different from all the others, and yet I was fearful. When we buried him in the ground, some people criticized me for not grieving loudly enough. It was not a question of sorrow. Of course I lamented, but I was prepared, almost expectant. There are occasions when death is a relief!

The physical response to impending doom passed, although the fear had not dissipated. I donned my coat and returned to the front of the house. Job was coming up the path. The sight of him, strong and confident, was immeasurably reassuring. I ran out the door and into his arms, catching him by surprise. He saw the torment on my face, and held me tightly, allowing his strength to flow into my body.

We walked arm in arm back up the path. Job, ever the patient one, waited for me to explain, but I could not speak. I could only savor his protection as a grape-vine enjoys the shadow of the watchman's tower.

Just as we sat down on the ground to talk, Job saw a messenger running up the hill. His body was covered with sweat and blood, and the distress on his face was of the kind that leaves a permanent mark. "The oxen were plowing and the donkeys were grazing nearby," he explained, "and the Sabeans attacked and carried the cattle off. They put the servants to the sword, and I am the only one who has escaped to tell you!"

Job turned white. Our farmers were good men, family men, productive workers. This was more than an economic loss. Curse the Sabeans! They were camel nomads, slave traders of the most despicable kind.

The first messenger had barely finished speaking when another runner arrived and said, "The fire of God fell from the sky and burned up the sheep and the servants, and I am the only one who has escaped to tell you!"

Fire of God? A lightning strike so awesome it could burn up seven thousand sheep and our faithful shepherds? Everything gone in one cosmic flash? An evil force was at large. I was sure of it.

There was more to come. Another messenger arrived, his blood-stained sword still in his hand. "The Chaldeans formed three raiding parties and swept down on your camels and carried them off. They put the servants to the sword, and I am the only one who has escaped to tell you!"

Oh, that must have been a terrible battle! Job required that all of our servants who worked beyond reach of the house be armed. Marauding bands were not uncommon. The Chaldeans, who directed their lives according to the patterns of the moon and stars, were a people born to make war. The Sabeans took slaves, but the Chaldeans slaughtered.

Job and I sat there like stones. Three calamities in as many minutes had left us numb. We simply had no more outrage left.

Then the fourth messenger came. "Your sons and daughters were feasting and drinking wine at the oldest brother's house," he reported, "when suddenly a mighty wind swept in from the desert and struck the four corners of the house. It collapsed on them and they are dead, and I am the only one who has escaped to tell you!"

At this, Job got up and tore his robe. I fainted.

Chapter 5

I awoke to feel a cool compress on my head. My servant, her eyes swollen with weeping, was sitting on the ground by my bed. When I was able to focus my eyes on her tear-stained face, I knew that I had not dreamed of the loss of my children. It had really happened.

I had grieved when I lost the child who was stillborn. A baby is a person, in the womb or out, and that child had been life in me for almost nine months. He was a boy, small compared to my other children, but, nevertheless, complete in every detail. I cried as they wrapped him for burial. The pungency of the spices sprinkled on the cloths made me sick. After they placed him in our family tomb — would he be lonely there by himself? — I mourned for many days.

Now I had lost ten children! Can grief be multiplied ten times or does the well of sorrow eventually reach that place from which no more sorrow can be drawn? I who had possessed such a zest for life had no desire for it now. I longed to die, to be relieved of the terrible pain that I felt I could not possibly bear.

What was the Lord doing by taking away everything we loved? I knew He always did what was best, but the knowing in my head was separated by a stone wall from the feeling in my heart.

"Where is Job?" I asked my servant. She informed me that he was worshiping the Lord! I was incredulous and yet not at all surprised. Of course, Job would take his loss to his sovereign Creator and Sustainer. I struggled to my feet and walked slowly to the place outside our home where Job regularly offered his sacrifices.

There was Job, his robe torn and his head shaven, lying prostrate on the ground and crying out, "Naked I came from my mother's womb, and naked I will depart. The Lord gave and the Lord has taken away; may the name of the Lord be praised." Job never charged God with any wrongdoing. Never.

I fell down beside him and worshiped. While Job's faith took the straight path, my faith twisted and turned, but we arrived at the same place. God had taken everything we had, but He had left us Himself and each other. I would not have to grieve alone. Job, who had been my strength all our married life, would be at my side to support and comfort.

How often we proclaim that our trust is totally in the Lord when we really are trusting in the Lord and . . . I said I trusted in the Lord to give us good crops. What I meant was I trusted in the Lord and our farmers to give us good crops. I trusted in the Lord for security, but I also trusted in our city government and the servants who guarded our property. Now I was trusting in the Lord for strength. The Lord and Job.

The Lord is my rock. He truly is. But when I said so then, I was not depending on the Lord alone. Job — my beloved husband, my friend, my warmth when the evenings are cold, my refreshment in the heat of the day — Job was my rock, the firm base on which my life was built. The Lord was always there, as One to whom I prayed, but it was Job who worked out the answers.

What would it be like to trust in the Lord without Job's support? I was about to find out, through an experience more loathsome and odious than any yet recorded in the history of mankind.

Chapter 6

When it comes to balancing the events of life, our God is incomparable. Here Job and I were, sunken into the depths of grief, prone to reliving all our happy times with the children, dwelling in the past, and we had to get out and work! We had lost everything, you see, a fact that did not make its impact until our store of food ran out.

I had gone to the grain jar for wheat to make bread and found a handful of kernels left. Our storehouse contained enough food for a month or so, but, when that ran out, what would we do? For the first time since our devastation, Job and I sat down and talked about the future rather than the past. We would need a field, a garden, a few sheep. With only six household servants left, it would be necessary for us to till the soil and plant the seeds. Perhaps someone whom Job had helped would give us a ram and a ewe (how naive we were!).

"Do you think you could weave some cloth?" Job asked one morning. There was the slightest trace of a smile on his lips. I knew that he was thinking of that first week when I had moved into his home. The new bride was going to impress her husband by making him a coat. Not that Job needed a coat, or me to make it, for he had servants with nothing else to do but transform the oily wool into garments for the entire household to wear.

But I wanted to impress my husband with something I had made myself. I would take advice from no one but proceeded to gather the necessary spindles of wool. I sat myself before a loom and started to work, soon creating a massive tangle of threads. The servants alternated between suppressed laughter and alarm at how this disaster was going to affect the demeanor of the young bride, and indeed the tranquility of the whole household!

Evidently a servant hurried to inform Job, who walked in quietly, gently (but very firmly) lifted me up, and carried me out to the pathway that led from the house to the mountains. Then we took a long walk, during which Job patiently explained my role as his wife. When we returned, a weaver was sitting at the loom, expertly meshing warp and woof into a handsome piece of cloth. Every visible reminder of my stubbornness and pride had been removed. How like Job to untangle the knots of my life!

Since then I had learned to weave, and I would weave again. We were not helpless. Ours had not been the life of wealth and ease, but wealth and work. Together we would use God's gifts of health and strength, and, with His blessing, make a fresh start. Job and I would weave a new life. Not a vast and multicolored drapery as we had had before, but a smaller, more sober piece exemplifying warmth rather than grandeur.

We had discussed the reason for our present state. Job believed that Satan had been behind it all, that for some purpose we could not understand, God had allowed him to ruin us. Perhaps it was a test of our love for God, or to point out a sin we had not confessed. Were we involved in a celestial power struggle which God would ultimately win? If so, why us?

Job was puzzled, but he did not question God. He still maintained his integrity, a model of virtue before the whole city. People were amazed! "Find yourself another god!" they cried. "What benefit has your devotion been for you?" Job resisted. Each day we worshiped, praising God for our lives, which was all that we had left.

It was our custom to arise at dawn, cleanse ourselves, and pray before our morning meal. Job always sprang out of bed, while I would savor the comfort of our robes a few more minutes. On this particular morning I found it harder than usual to get up. I had had a restless night, marked by fearful dreams and finally a nightmare that left me in a cold sweat. Had someone or something been standing by our bed, or had I imagined it all? That sense of the nearness of a sinister force, which had preceded the loss of everything we possessed, again clutched my heart.

Job had not arisen either. He was not feeling well, he said. I could not recall when he had last been sick and thought it strange that he should be ill this morning, when he had been in perfect health the night before. Job spoke of a numbness in his feet. I boiled some water and herbs for a poultice. When I bent down to apply the steaming cloths, I was truly alarmed. Job's feet were swollen, covered with large sores that oozed pus. He cried out in pain when I touched him.

Within an hour Job's entire body was covered with these hideous boils. I knew what leprosy was, of course, for we had lepers outside the city, and often ministered to their needs. But if this disease was leprosy — and I wasn't sure — I had never heard of it progressing so swiftly. Job even had the cursed swellings on his head!

I feared for Job's sanity. I feared for his life. And then, another realization struck me. If people in the city found out, Job would be forced to live as an outcast, shunned by everyone, an odious creature required by law to roam the dung hills and garbage dumps beyond the city wall. Could I protect him from the ever-curious eyes of the townspeople? Could I hide such an illustrious citizen until the disease ran its course, or worse, a possibility I refused to face?

While I was devising schemes of secret confinement, Job rose and walked toward the door. "Where are you going?" I screamed in a voice devoid of any comfort or love.

"I am going to Mazbalah, where I belong," Job replied.

Mazbalah! The place of ashes! Job, ever virtuous, was going as a volunteer!

I stumbled after him as he slowly made his way along the path. In silence we walked, skirting the city, with our heads bowed low. The few people who saw us drew back in horror. One man, who had sat with Job at the gates, cried, "Unclean! Unclean!" We knew without looking up that he would spread the word: "Let me tell you what has happened to Job, our great civic leader!"

The winter rains had reduced the dung and rubbish to a solid, compact mass of earth. Mazbalah was a hill of stench and litter of everything that could not be burned. One spot was no better than another, so Job just sat down amidst a pile of broken pottery. While I gazed in disgust, he picked up a piece of jar and began scraping himself, the pus and blood forming an orange paste that enshrouded his entire body.

It was then that I broke. I could not bear the sight of him suffering so, and, yes, looking so hideous even my love could not blind me to his total revulsion. "Are you still holding on to your integrity?" I asked, in a voice so bitter it made vinegar sweet. "Curse God and die!"

Out of that bulbous face peered Job's eyes, saddened much more by my rejection than by the physical suffering that tormented his every nerve. He replied, "You are talking like a foolish woman. Shall we accept good from God, and not trouble?"

In all this, Job did not sin in what he said. He just sat there, a beautiful man on a dung heap. I wept until the ashes at my feet were drenched with my tears.

Chapter 7

D o I sound like a bitter woman? I had not been so before Job's affliction. Is bitterness a seed that lies dormant within us until it is nourished? The Ancients say that we are born with sinful natures, only controlled by the Spirit of God. I was emptied of God's Spirit. My Creator and Lord seemed as far away as the stars in the heavens.

One night, after all the children were in bed, Job took me out to the rim of the ridge. The sky was so clear we could see into the very hearts of the stars. Job pointed out the Bear, Orion, the Pleiades, and the constellations in the southern sky. God had stretched out the heavens to make room for them all. He was as distant as the stars, and yet as close as the beating of my heart.

Now I felt abandoned by God. I could not find Him in my heart, nor in the sky, obscured day and night by the smoke from the fires of Mazbalah. Nor could I find Job within that figure of rotting flesh sitting among the ashes and scraping his legs with a shard of clay.

Yes, I was bitter, for we had also been abandoned by our friends. People we had known for years, who had shared the food at our table, simply disappeared. How I longed for an arm around my shoulder, a sympathizing word! Those with whom Job had counseled at the city gates came to stare or to laugh, but one visit was enough. Even our most trusted servants could not stand the sight of him.

One day some bullies from the town ventured close enough to jeer. "What do you say, holy man? Where is your God? Is He hiding under the garbage on the left? Or rising with the stink of the dung on the right? Perhaps He's been burned up and blown away." How they laughed! A big, coarse man came up and struck Job on his cheek. The welt simply melded into the rest of his disfigurement.

Job had three special friends, Eliphaz, Bildad, and Zophar, men he had known for years. Although they had moved away from our city, Job had kept in touch via the caravans that regularly traversed the desert. When the news of Job's troubles reached them, they set out from their homes, met together, and by agreement came to sympathize with him and comfort him. Isn't it ironic that our friends close by did nothing, yet these three men, who lived at such a distance, cared enough to leave their homes for our sakes?

Job was sitting in his usual place when his three friends came over the hill from the city gate. At first they could hardly recognize him. Job, who had always been so particular about his appearance, who had worn the finest robes, was dressed in rags. But as they came closer, it was the sores all over his body that brought them to their knees. They began to weep aloud. They tore their robes and sprinkled dust on their heads. As ones mourning the dead, they sat on the ground with Job for seven days and seven nights.

No one said a word to him, because they saw how great his suffering was. I sat there too, reflecting that if I had to choose between words and presence in a time of sorrow, I would choose presence. Why do we always think we have to speak?

Chapter 8

I s it not a characteristic of human nature that when we have triumphed over a crisis we are most vulnerable to Satan? Following a great victory there will be a setback. Our spiritual reserve, which is not inexhaustible, is finally spent, leaving us vulnerable to the mildest assaults.

So it was with Job, whose most difficult and trying time was not in the past, but in the future. After all that had happened, Job had remained true to God. Perhaps he now had a false sense of his spirituality, causing him to think he had arrived at the very end of his journey with God. After all, he had been stripped naked in soul and body, so what further test could be devised?

After a week, Job spoke, with words so laden with bitterness and despair that I could not believe they were coming out of his mouth. The musing, arguing, and debating that were going on in his very bowels were suddenly exposed to our view. I no more wanted to see the inside of my husband than I wanted to see the outside!

Job cursed the day he was born. Incredulous! With a holy lust he had loved every day of his life. Now he was asking why he had not perished at birth, dying as he came out of the womb. "Why were there knees to receive me and breasts that I might be nursed?" he asked. God had allowed his father to place his new-born son across his knees as a token that he accepted the responsibility of his parentage. God had caused his mother to produce the sweetest milk on earth to flow into his waiting mouth. Better the baby had gone to rest with the great and famous dead, concluded Job. In the ground the wicked cease from turmoil and the weary are at rest.

We had lost a son who never knew trouble. Had we rejoiced then? Ah, no. For he would never see the first rays of dawn, nor the evening stars. If we shield our children from the ugliness of life, we cloak the beauty as well. Would any parent desire for her child, fresh from the womb, the freedom of death rather than the bondage of life? I do not think so.

Job had a question: "Why is light given to those in misery, and life to the bitter of soul, to those who long for death that does not come, who search for it more than for hidden treasure, who are filled with gladness and rejoice when they reach the grave?" Who can explain why God keeps open those eyes that want to be shut? Here he was, searching for death more than a man searches for hidden treasure, and God would not let him find it.

How thin Job was! Like a barley stalk, withered and bent. He would not eat, but sighed and groaned by the hour. Nor could he sleep. In a mood of confession he cried out, "What I feared has come upon me; what I dreaded has happened to me. I have no peace, no quietness; I have no rest, but only turmoil."

I could not blame Job for being completely involved with himself. When we are sorely afflicted, we do not naturally reach out to others. Perhaps we cannot reach out to God. We cannot reflect on what His purpose might be, what He is trying to teach us, what we must lose in order that we might gain.

My own pain was deep. My heart was broken, but my body was whole. Satan knows how tied we are to our bodies. A man will give all he has for his own life; but strike his flesh and bones, and he can quickly curse God to His face. Did Job have a breaking point? As time wore on, would he lose his integrity?

I looked at the three friends sitting there on the ground. If ever there were an opportunity to offer comfort, it was now.

Chapter 9

S ince Eliphaz was the oldest of the three men, he was privileged to speak first. I had met Eliphaz on several occasions and always found him a considerate gentleman, composed and dignified. Temanites are renowned for their wisdom, which amazes me, considering that they come from the stock of Esau, and Eliphaz tried to live up to that reputation.

Job had described Eliphaz as a mystic, one who seeks an inner experience with God. He was always talking about dreams and visions, as if that were a sufficient measurement of a person's religion. This was hard for down-to-earth Job to take, and the discussions around the fire had always been lively. Polite, of course, but lively.

Eliphaz's response to Job's despondent outbreak started off on an encouraging note. He reminded him of how he had instructed so many people, how he had strengthened feeble hands, how his words had supported those who stumbled, and how he had strength-

ened feeble knees. This was all true, but Eliphaz
couldn't stop there.

"But now trouble comes to you, and you are dis-
couraged," he went on. "It strikes *you*, and you are dis-
mayed. Should not your piety be your confidence and
your blameless ways your hope?" In other words, what
Job had done for others, he could not do for himself!

It was Eliphaz's view that no one innocent had
ever perished, and no one upright had ever been destroyed. Therefore, there must be some small matter in
which Job had offended the Almighty. If he was reap-
ing evil, he must have sown it. Eliphaz had had another one of his dreams, vivid enough to make his hair
stand on end, he said, in which a form had stood before his eyes and asked in a hushed voice, "Can a mortal be more righteous than God? Can a man be more
pure than his Maker?" If God charges His angels with
error, how much more faulty and frail are those on
earth. They are crushed more readily than a moth.

Eliphaz's view, that the reason for Job's suffering
was his unconfessed sin, was simply not true. It was
not my place to protest, but my heart cried out, "No!
No!" Job's face revealed his anguish, but he remained
silent as Eliphaz had more to say. Eliphaz usually had
more to say!

"Hardship does not spring from the soil, nor does
trouble sprout from the ground," claimed Eliphaz. Men
act after the impulses of their evil nature and bring affliction upon themselves. "Man is born to trouble as

surely as sparks fly upward," he said, giving the fire a strong poke.

So what is the sinful man to do? Appeal to God. Lay the cause before Him. God performs wonders that cannot be fathomed, miracles that cannot be counted. He bestows rain on the earth; He sends water upon the countryside. God offers hope to the poor and needy, while restraining the crafty schemers who would like to get them in their clutches.

Eliphaz looked upon Job's condition as discipline from the Almighty. No comfort in that supposition! Then he went on to tell Job that God who wounds, also binds up; He injures, but He also heals. Eliphaz then had the presumption to offer rescue and restoration, on the basis of another vision, I presume. "You will laugh at destruction and famine," he said. "You will know that your tent is secure; you will take stock of your property and find nothing missing. You will know that your children will be many" (our *children*, he said), "and your descendants like the grass of the earth. You will come to the grave in full vigor, like sheaves gathered in season."

Well, these were beautiful words and meant to be comforting, I guess; but if these blessings were based upon Job's confession of a sin he hadn't committed, they were no comfort at all. I have little respect for people who promise relief and restoration to sufferers with some sort of prescription; and then, when the prescription fails, it is because the patient hasn't carried it out properly or because the disease was too deep-seated to cure. Never the fault of the prescription!

I wondered, too, how much Eliphaz had suffered. Could he give testimony to a personal experience which applied the religious knowledge he had heard whispered in his ears during those dreams? Experience can be equated to religion, which makes both the experience and the religion poor. I could find nothing in all that Eliphaz said that suggested to me he saw himself as a sinner-sufferer, or that his religious experiences drew him nearer to God.

I waited for Job to respond.

Chapter 10

S trange, how a woman can be married to a man for years, decades even, and not really know him. You think you can identify every mole on your husband's body, and all of a sudden you discover that he doesn't like goat meat, but he thought your feelings would be hurt if he said so, or he's really afraid of thunderstorms because he was frightened by one when he was a little boy.

I had been married to Job since I was thirteen. Ours was an exceptional marriage, since Job took no concubines. We were very close, two vines twining around each other. Job did not isolate me from his world: he shared with me his conversations at the city gates and his administration of the farmers and herdsmen. I sought Job's counsel on management of our household. Together we reared the children.

So it was, that Job's reply to Eliphaz caught me by surprise. It was not his physical condition that was tormenting Job, although he certainly felt pain. Job's anguish came from his belief that his suffering was undeserved and from the refusal of his friends to accept this. "If all my misery was placed on the scales, it would surely outweigh the sand of the seas," Job cried. "The arrows of the Almighty are in me, my spirit drinks in their poison; God's terrors are marshaled against me."

Violent pain is easier to endure than drawn-out mental suffering. The pain of birthing is as nothing compared to the pain of having birthed a wayward child. I who had been given such wholeness of body and spirit could not empathize with Job in his condition. Indeed, my sympathy was less than genuine because of a callousness I didn't want to admit. How easy it is to prescribe feelings for another person when you have never been in his situation!

I realized that Job had lost his spiritual appetite. His soul was like food eaten without salt, or the flavorless white of an egg. He was weary of life and saw no prospects for any relief. After all, he was not made of stone or bronze. He had no strength or power to help himself.

To add to Job's despair was the position taken by his three friends. I shared his disappointment. Like the intermittent streams that are gorged with melting snow in the winter but cease to flow in the dry season and eventually vanish from the wadis, the friends were no help when refreshment was needed. Job was like a caravan of Tema looking for water and finding only the arid wasteland. He had not asked them for money or even deliverance, only honest words, and all they could give him was condemnation. Job had every right to remind them of his righteousness.

Meanwhile, his disease continued unabated. He hardly slept. His skin was broken and festering, with scabs covered with so many worms he seemed to be clothed in a moving coat. He was so repulsive I could not look at him, much less touch his loathsome flesh.

Surrounded as he was by four mute, squatting figures, Job opened his heart to God. Some might call his words blasphemy, but God's people should always be willing to be completely frank with their heavenly Father. Job could share his bitterness as well as his praise, his perplexity as well as his confidence.

"My days are swifter than a weaver's shuttle," Job began, thinking again of our looms which had produced such beautiful cloth, "and they come to an end without hope. Remember, O God, that my life is but a breath; my eyes will never see happiness again." (Looking at his red-rimmed eyes, full of yellow matter, I wondered if Job would ever see *anything* again.)

Job believed that he soon would be in his grave. He had to speak out while he had time. He had to ask God why He frightened him with terrifying dreams and visions, why He was acting like a spy, raking sin to the surface. "Let me alone!" he pleaded. "My days have no meaning."

"What is man that You make so much of him, that You give him so much attention, that You examine

him every morning, and test him every moment? Let
me alone!" he pleaded again.

Why had God made Job His target? Was he a bur-
den to God? Job did not understand God's intentions,
nor do any of us, really. We all hate to admit that we
have to accept God without knowing His immediate
purposes or how they fit into the eternal scheme of
things. Isn't faith a condition of having questions for
which God declines to give the answers?

Job asked to be pardoned for his offenses, whatever
they might be, for he believed he would soon lie down
in the dust and be no more. Being too exhausted to
speak further, he lowered his head and stared into the
debris around his feet.

Chapter 11

B ildad the Shuhite was now ready to give his point of view. I could tell by the way he cleared his throat that he felt he had something important to say. Bildad regarded himself as a scholar, a depository of the wisdom of the Ancients. He may have had wisdom and experience, but I always found him to be a man without tenderness. In an hour of crisis do we want true doctrine or true love?

"How long will you say such things?" he asked Job. "Your words are a blustering wind." So much for comfort. "Does God pervert justice? Does the Almighty pervert what is right?" There was the old accusation again. If Job was stricken, he deserved to be — he must have done something wrong.

Bildad made me so angry I wanted to strike him on the mouth, but when he brought our dead children into the argument, I was appalled. Bildad made the claim that our children had sinned against God and so God gave them over to the penalty of their sin. They must have been guilty of some heinous deed to be so sud-

denly swept out of life. I couldn't believe we were
hearing such words.

Of course, Bildad had the solution. Job should
plead his case before the Almighty. If Job was so pure
and upright, God would rouse Himself and restore him
to his rightful place. I readily admit I was puzzled by
God's action, but I never thought He was sleeping. I
also did not like Bildad's inference that Job had a case
to plead. Calamity is no proof of guilt in those on
whom it falls. Evil in the hand of God may serve a
wider use than the chastisement of one person.

Then the "great scholar" told Job that if he sought
God, God would restore him to his rightful place and
give him a prosperous future. This was a lovely promise, but it was based on Bildad's belief that Job had
sinned against God.

While Eliphaz centered upon emotion, Bildad ap-
pealed to tradition. "Ask the former generations and
find out what their fathers learned, for we were born
only yesterday and know nothing, and our days on
earth are but a shadow. Will they not instruct you and
tell you? Will they not bring forth words from their
understanding?"

Bildad had lived for some time in Egypt. His land
holdings bordered the Nile River, a fact he liked to
remind us of. The soil there is very fertile, in contrast
to our rocky land, which will produce good crops but
only with much coaxing. It was natural, therefore, for
Bildad to use the papyrus plant as an example of a

person who forgets God: he perishes like a reed without water. Or tear a flourishing plant from its place in the garden and it quickly withers. The place where it grew disowns it and says, "I never knew you." Such is the fate of the evildoer, for God's grace is withdrawn from him.

However, God does not reject a blameless man or strengthen the hands of evildoers. "He will yet fill your mouth with laughter and your lips with shouts of joy. Your enemies will be clothed in shame, and the tents of the wicked will be no more." These words of encouragement revealed the fact that Bildad did indeed love Job in his way. I was ready to forgive him his dogmatism if he could offer to Job the hope that his lips encrusted with sores would someday laugh again, or that his heart so heavy with grief would find reason to generate shouts of joy.

Yes, I also wanted to see our enemies get their due. If God chose to wipe out their homes, it would be fine with me. I am not a vindictive person and would not bring down destruction on anyone's head, but I would not weep if those around us, who had seen our plight and left us to bear it alone, fell under the wrath of a divine Judge.

I have observed that the greater one's troubles, the fewer friends there are willing to help. When we have experienced the ultimate state of disaster and have no one, then we are compelled to rely on God alone, which is the supreme spiritual condition. Good can come out of bad, I conclude, so Bildad's promise of restoration might come true.

Job was considering Bildad's speech. "Whose words are a blustering wind?" I wanted to ask.

Chapter 12

I remember a night when we were awakened from a sound sleep by an uneasiness we could not at first identify. My immediate thought was that Job was shaking me, but then I realized that the ground beneath us was heaving. Pots were falling from their shelves, vegetables and fruit were strewn everywhere, and our doorway was suddenly a doorway no more.

We could hear the children screaming, augmented by cries of alarm from the servants. "Earthquake!" Job said, grabbing my hand. We wanted to go to the children, but that was impossible. Only the earth was allowed to move. We lay together, rolling against each other until the ground was steady once more.

Job listened politely to Bildad. He agreed that God would not reject a blameless man, yet he felt rejected and he believed he was blameless. The question remained: How can a mortal be righteous before God? Job could argue with God all he wanted, but he knew he could not come out of such a dispute unscathed.

God is free to do whatever He likes because He is
God. He can shake the earth as He did the night of the
earthquake, or He can speak to the sun so it does not
shine. He performs wonders that cannot be fathomed,
miracles that cannot be numbered. Can a God such as
this be challenged? Could Job go up to Him and say,
"What are you doing?" No, Job could only plead for a
hearing, and after that rely upon God's mercy and
judgment, however they might interplay.

As I was sitting there on the dung in the awful
stench listening to Job, I thought his spirit had reached
the lowest abyss in its alienation from God. He was a
broken man. To hear him say that he had no concern
for himself, that he despised his own life — "The
blameless and the wicked are all the same to God" —
was not the Job I knew.

But then, it was as if Job didn't see Bildad, Zophar,
Eliphaz, or me at all. He began to talk to God in the
direct way that had always been his custom. "My days
are swifter than a runner; they fly away without a
glimpse of joy. They skim past like boats of papyrus,
like eagles swooping down on their prey." Job too had
seen Egypt (remember that, Bildad!) and had been im-
pressed by the papyrus boats with their upturned bows
that sailed a hundred miles or more from the delta of
the Nile to Gaza.

Job was always open with God. He could admit his
feelings. He could confess that he was puzzled, because he knew God never rejected a man because he

was honest. "If I say, 'I will forget my complaint, I will change my expression, and smile,' I still dread all my sufferings, for I know You will not hold me innocent." Since Job felt that he was already found guilty, why should he struggle in vain? "Even if I washed myself with soap and my hands with washing soda, You would plunge me into a slime pit so that even my clothes would detest me."

God was not a man whom Job could confront in court. There was no mediator to arbitrate between Job and God. There was no one to remove God's rod of correction. Job's despondency was so deep he could give free rein to his complaint and speak out in the bitterness of his soul. Life couldn't be any more loathsome, could it?

The old questions again surfaced. What charges did God have against Job? Why did He seemingly smile on the schemes of the wicked and oppress a man who was not guilty of sin? As if God needed reminding, Job said, "Your hands shaped me and made me. Will You now turn and destroy me? Remember that You molded me like clay. Will You now turn me to dust again?"

Job had always been intimately involved in the work of our farm. He would tuck up his tunic and join the servants shearing sheep or pruning the grapevines. He had slaughtered animals by the hundreds, so when he asked God, "Did You not pour me out like milk and curdle me like cheese, clothe me with skin and flesh and knit me together with bones and sinews?" these experiences were firmly in his mind.

Job acknowledged that God had given him life, but now he wondered why. He was so full of shame, drowned in his affliction, feeling hunted by God. It seemed that God was sending forces against him in waves, and yet he believed he was an innocent man. Job wished he had died before he was born, or had been born and carried straight from the womb to the grave.

Job felt that he was almost dead, and I, seeing him so tortured, so emaciated, so diseased, wondered myself how much more he could endure. At that moment I did not look upon his death with dread. It would be a relief, not only for Job but for me! You may consider me callous or selfish, looking out only for myself. Not so! I only admit to a feeling that many have had. There is a proper time and place for death. We need not feel guilty about accepting the inevitable.

What happens to us after we die? God has not told us much about that. We know that it is a place of no return; once we go there we never come back. Job saw it as a land of gloom and deep shadow, a land of deepest night, of deep shadow and disorder, where even the light is like darkness. This was a weary Job speaking. The Ancient Ones tell us if we have faith in God we will not be separated from him, and Job believed it.

He had talked a long time, so passionately he had completely expended the little energy that he had. Now he lay down on the ashes, too weary to raise his head or even open his eyes. I looked at the faces of the three friends. Zophar was anxious to speak, I could tell.

What more needed to be said?

Chapter 13

I n my opinion, Zophar was dogmatic to the point of
arrogance. When he came by for a visit, I kept myself as busy as possible. I expected nothing comforting
from his words this time, and I was not disappointed.

Zophar liked to talk in questions, so he began that
way. "Are all these words to go unanswered?" he
asked. "Is this talker to be vindicated?" Zophar felt it
was his duty to speak up and rebuke Job, whom he
accused of mocking God. He wished that God would
speak and reveal the secrets of wisdom, but since He
did not, Zophar considered himself a worthy substitute.

It was Zophar's opinion that no one could fathom
the mysteries of God. No one could probe His limits.
They were higher than the heavens and deeper than the
depths of the grave, longer than the earth and wider
than the sea. Certainly Job and I agreed with him
there, but to us God's mysteries were delights that only
increased our love for Him.

One day a trader of gems had come by, his heavily
guarded bags full of rubies and sapphires. He laid his

bundles on a robe spread out for that purpose, un-
wrapped layer after layer of soft cloth, and finally revealed jewels so brilliant as to take your breath away.
Job held a ruby up to the light, letting the sun's rays
break the deep red into a thousand beams. "Who can
explain the creation of such magnificence?" he asked
the trader. "Only God could make such beauty!" This
was obviously a new idea to the merchant.

Zophar went on with his questions. "If God comes
along and confines you in prison and convenes a court,
who can oppose Him? Surely He recognizes deceitful
men; and when He sees evil, does He not take note?"
It was Zophar's contention that if Job would only de-
vote his heart to God, and stretch out his hands to
Him, if he would only put away the sin that was in his
hand and allow no evil to dwell in his tent, then he
could lift up his face without shame; he could stand
firm and without fear.

Zophar was absolutely sure that Job would forget
his trouble, recalling it only as waters gone by, if he
would only admit to his sin. Security, hope, rest,
peace, popularity — all these would be Job's.

But what if Job hadn't sinned against God? Zophar
didn't have the answer. To him, every doubt and diffi-
culty was a sign of sin. So Job had to defend himself,
drawing upon mental and physical resources that taxed
him to the limit. I sat among the shards, marveling that
he could reason at all, much less with any pique.

Job's mind was still sharp. I was encouraged at the force of his response. "Doubtless you are the people, and wisdom will die with you! But I have a mind as well as you." (Hurrah for you, Job!) "I am not inferior to you. Who does not know all these things?"

There was enough spunk left in Job to cause him to point out the superficiality of his friends' advice. They thought they could unravel the complexities of his situation with a few old maxims that represented nothing but a shallow religiosity. What did they know of suffering? Job the righteous had become a laughingstock to his friends, men at ease who were contemptible of misfortune. While Job slipped into deeper distress, these so-called friends carried on, undisturbed and secure. Being despised by his friends was one of the most painful things Job had to bear.

Job pointed out to the three advisers huddled together on the garbage heaps of Mazbalah that the hand of the Lord controlled breath and life. Even the animals and birds knew that. To God belong wisdom and power; counsel and understanding are His. God is omnipotent. If He holds back the waters, there is drought; if He lets them loose, they devastate the land.

As for those in positions of influence, God controls them too, both the deceived and the deceiver. Counselors, judges, kings, priests, advisers, elders — all can be stripped and silenced. Nations and their leaders become great and are subsequently destroyed. The proud are humbled. Eliphaz, Bildad, and Zophar had all seen this happen. Job had seen it, too. He was not inferior to them.

Job did not want to debate his situation with the three men. He wanted to argue his case with God. If he could but speak to the Almighty, he would be satisfied.

Where was God? Have you ever asked that question? Job and I knew that God was everywhere, but we yearned for evidence of His presence — a sound, a touch. All around us was nothing but smoking waste. Oh, if we could experience again a divine fire!

Chapter 14

As far as Job was concerned, the maxims of his friends were proverbs of ashes. Job knew proverbs, and he certainly knew ashes! They had yet to say anything he did not already know. As for being physicians, their medicine was worthless. If they really wanted to help Job, the best thing they could do would be to stop talking. That would be real wisdom.

Job did not think the three men could speak honestly on God's behalf. After all, what would be the outcome if God examined them? They weren't perfect! Job was so confident of his own innocence he dared to go before God with the assurance that he would be vindicated.

There were only two things that Job wanted God to do: withdraw His hand from him, and stop frightening him with His terrors. He felt like a leaf, tormented by the wind, chased here and there, and never allowed to settle down. Job had atoned for his past sins. They were forgiven long ago. Was God now dredging up the sins of his youth? Job vacillated between hope and despair.

Spring on our hillsides is fleeting. One day there are wildflowers blooming everywhere. Then the summer heat rolls in and they are no more. Life is like that, isn't it? A person springs up like a flower and in a few days withers away. But we have troubles the flower never knows. Pink flax or purple anemones (my favorite) cannot anticipate death. We know our days are determined by God. He has set the limits of our months, and there is nothing we can do to change that.

A tree, on the other hand, has hope. If it is cut down, it will sprout again, and its new shoots will not fail. The stump may look dead, but give it some water and branches appear. Not so man. Once he dies he will not rise again. Wouldn't it be wonderful if we could just go to sleep when God was angry with us and stay that way until He felt favorable, then be renewed? I should like that!

If a man dies, will he live again? All the days of our hard service we wait for our release to come. Job and I have often talked about life after death. We know that God will remember us in the grave. In His mind which has no limitations, He will long for the creatures His hands have made. He will call us, and we will answer, our offenses sealed up in a bag where God will not keep track of them.

Some say God sends man away, all hope destroyed, but perpetuates his soul through his children. While we are glad our immortality is assured in this way, we will not know it. We will not see what happens to our children, but only feel the pain of our own bodies and only mourn for ourselves. What consolation is this?

Eliphaz interrupted at this point. He was old enough to be Job's father, a fact which made him exceedingly touchy about accepting any wisdom from Job. Eliphaz began by accusing Job of undermining piety, of hindering devotion to God. He compared Job's words with the sirocco, the hot east wind that turns the earth into an oven. Like everyone in our region, I have seen the sirocco make the mildest-mannered person irritable, snapping at other people for no reason. Oh, the dust that penetrates every crevice of house and person! How we would clean when the great wind passed! (I began by blowing my nose.)

A good summary of what Eliphaz had to say is the question: "Who do you think you are to question God?" How can a mere man, vile and corrupt, who drinks up evil like water, vent his rage against God? For Eliphaz, Job's suffering was due to his sin, and that was that. He went back to the gray-haired sages again: they knew that man suffers torment because he shakes his fist at God. Eliphaz shook his fist in Job's face just to emphasize his point.

Such depressing counsel, all this talk about ruin and darkness. Eliphaz was like a lioness holding her kitten in her teeth: he just would not let go of his belief that Job was unrighteous, and therefore getting what he deserved. "Though his face is covered with fat and his waist bulges with flesh, he will inhabit ruined towns and houses where no one lives, houses crumbling to rubble," he said, making direct reference to our former prosperity. "He will no longer be rich and his wealth will not endure, nor will his possessions spread over the land."

Eliphaz described the unrighteous man (Job?) as a vine stripped of its unripe grapes, an olive tree shedding its blossoms. What pictures came to my mind! I longed to see our gardens again, the clusters of purple fruit on the vines, fragrant white flowers forming a halo over the tree. Oh, to be in the hills again, rather than here in a world that was totally black, where nothing grew but rats.

Eliphaz was finished. Job shifted his position, picked up a shard, and assiduously began working on a huge boil that had erupted just above his ankle. He was taking his time before responding.

Chapter 15

When Job finally spoke, he accused his three "friends" of being miserable comforters. (Under my breath I said, "Good for you!") Their long-winded speeches and endless arguments were as irritating and useless as the flies buzzing about our heads. If Job had been in their place, his mouth would have offered encouragement and comfort.

Job was feeling the sting of God's rebuke as well. His picture of God was a beast of prey who had seized him by the neck and was tearing him to shreds with sharp teeth. He had no friends, no household, no God, indeed mankind itself was his enemy. And what about me? I had become part of the surroundings, another heap of ashes. Why not? I was repulsed like all the rest.

From time to time men from town would come out to Mazbalah to jeer and throw stones. One bully dared his friend to *touch* Job, which he did by drawing his fingernail across Job's cheek. The blood which flowed quickly mingled with the soot and pus, creating a ghoulish mosaic that made me retch.

Now Job pictured God as an archer, piercing his kidneys and spilling his gall on the ground. "Again and again He bursts upon me; He rushes at me like a warrior." It was such a hopeless situation, from Job's point of view.

The Arabs have a custom of sewing themselves up into a garment so that it cannot be removed without ripping a seam. I do not know why they do this (I have never understood Arabs), but Job felt as though he were sewn up inside his suffering. Indeed, he looked terrible, eyes red with weeping, deep shadows under his eyes. Would God ever cut his seam of sorrow?

Job's hands had been free of violence. His prayer had been pure. And yet God had not responded to his appeal. Perhaps if he had an advocate, an intercessor who would plead with God on his behalf? Oh, how Job longed for a friend, but not one like the three miserable men sitting on their haunches amidst the refuse of a hundred generations!

"Only a few years will pass before I go on the journey of no return," Job said quietly. "My spirit is broken, my days are cut short, the grave awaits me."

Must he suffer like this for a few *years?* I wondered. *What does "few" mean?* Oh, I did not want Job to die, and yet, I did not want him to live on like this. He had been surrounded by hostility, spat upon, despised by supposedly righteous men who were really hypocrites.

We had made so many plans, Job and I. Like all parents, we had dreams for our children, we had hopes and ambitions for our home. Now the only home we could hope for was the grave. My future was as bleak as Job's, for without him I had nothing. I *was* nothing. Job expressed it so well when he said, "If I say to corruption, 'You are my father,' and to the worm, 'my mother' or 'my sister,' where then is my hope?" Would hope go with us to the gates of death? Would it descend with us into the dust?

I knew it would not.

Chapter 16

E very time I listened to Bildad, I felt sorry for his
wife. I could just picture him sitting in front of
his house, droning on about the same old things, the
most boring husband on this whole earth. I bet if a
caravan from the east pulled up with something new in
women's wear, Bildad wouldn't even let his wife look.
"The old styles were good enough for my mother," he
would argue, "They're good enough for you." The poor
woman was probably running around in animal hides.

Bildad's great advice to Job was, "Be sensible." As
if Job hadn't been sensible! He just couldn't agree with
Bildad that his misfortune was due to his sin. Perhaps
the wisdom of the past taught that for every effect
there is a cause, but Job did not believe that was true
in his case. It was not wisdom that he desired from
Bildad, anyway, but compassion. Didn't Bildad have
any *feelings*? Could he offer nothing but tradition as a
solution to Job's problem?

When we are in anguish do we want advice, or do
we want someone to hold us tightly and soothe us with

words of comfort? Here was Bildad ranting on about snares of the wicked, when all Job wanted was for him to say, "I am your friend. I love you." He didn't need Bildad to tell him that terrors startle him on every side, that calamity eats away parts of the skin. He could see into his own body through the gaping holes in his flesh.

Bildad replaced rationality with cruelty when he told Job that the wicked person has no offspring or descendants among his people, no survivor where once he lived. To lay the death of our ten children at Job's feet was heartless, and it was simply not true. But Bildad was a gushing stream that could not stop flowing. He went on to say that men of the west are appalled at the fate of the wicked. Men of the east are seized with horror. Was that the opinion of the whole countryside? Did everyone regard Job as a man who didn't know God?

These insinuations had a devastating effect upon Job's spirit. "How long will you torment me and crush me with words?" he asked. "Ten times now you have reproached me; shamelessly you attack me. If it is true that I have gone astray, my error remains my concern alone."

I picked at the dirt between my toes and whispered "Amen."

Job's quandary was not with Bildad; it was with *God*. Why didn't God respond to his cries? Job tried to go in one direction and God was blocking his path. He tried to go another way and God shrouded it in darkness. Job had no honor, no vestige of worth. He was a great tree torn up by its roots.

Loneliness is one of life's saddest conditions. Alienation is another. Job was completely friendless, forgotten by kinsmen, acquaintances, servants, everyone. Why hadn't his relatives come? By now they must have heard the news. They could have made the trip. Where were all the guests to whom we had given food and lodging? "If you ever need anything, just ask," they had said. How shallow their promises! As for servants, those trusted few who had been spared death, they looked upon us as strangers. Job had summoned his personal man many times, but he would not come. Job had begged him, and the man obstinately refused even to come near the dung heaps.

I was disappointed, but I also understood. Job's appearance was so loathsome I was barely able to endure him myself. His stench was enough to make anyone gag. Rotting flesh, whether it's on a live man or a dead one, has the same putrefying odor. Job was nothing but skin and bones. He said himself that he had escaped with only the skin of his teeth — next to nothing.

There we all sat, ourselves absorbing the odor of human manure. "Have pity on me, my friends, have pity," Job pleaded, "for the hand of God has struck me. Why do you pursue me as God does? Will you never get enough of my flesh?" Eliphaz, Bildad, and Zophar — cannibals who feasted on human arms and legs!

Job's eyes fell upon the shreds of skin hanging
from his arms. The body is such a transitory thing.
Would anyone remember him, the person, that existed
apart from a physical being? "Oh, that my words were
recorded, that they were written on a scroll, that they
were inscribed with an iron tool on lead, or engraved
in rock forever!"

Yes, we needed an indelible record carved in rock,
that it might stand as a perpetual witness to all generations: "This is what happened to the heart and body of
a man named Job."

There was a past to be remembered, but there was
a future too. Job reflected again upon God as his
goel, his Vindicator and Witness. "I know that my
Redeemer lives," he declared, "and in the end He will
stand upon the earth. And after my skin has been destroyed" (that time didn't seem so very far away),
"yet in my flesh I will see God; I myself will see
Him with my own eyes — I, and not another. How my
heart yearns within me!"

What did human vindication matter, when Job's
controversy was with God? Someday this estrangement
would cease. Job would behold God's face. He would
find peace. "Oh, Job, my beloved," I cried out, "you
will have communion with God again! He will clear
your name before the whole world!" I wept at his dec-
laration of faith.

As for those who had hounded Job with false accusations, who had insisted that the root of all his trouble

lay in him, Job had a few words to say. "You should fear the sword yourselves," he warned them, "for wrath will bring punishment by the sword, and then you will know that there is judgment." God does indeed deal with injustice. God's appearance would bring joy to Job, but terror to those who fastened false charges of guilt upon him.

I sensed in Job a turning point. The strain had been relieved. Now he could think more calmly; he could set his sufferings in a wider framework. He slumped face forward into the blackened waste. Whether he fainted or simply fell into an exhausted sleep, I do not know.

Chapter 17

Job awakened after a while, weak but lucid. If he expected a respite from the interminable words of his friends, he was mistaken. Zophar could hardly wait to speak.

Zophar was the most dogmatic person I have ever met. He liked to think he was espousing godly doctrine, but he was really giving his own opinion in an absolute way. He was fixed and inflexible, a prisoner of his own assertions. I could not imagine him and his wife sitting down and talking about *anything*. I pictured her as a spineless woman who had long since stopped having any ideas of her own. My Job acknowledged that I had a brain, and I loved him for that.

"Surely you know how it has been from of old, ever since man was placed on the earth," Zophar began, "that the mirth of the wicked is brief, the joy of the godless lasts but a moment." (Yes, we knew that.) "A man's pride can reach to the heavens; his head touch a cloud, but he will perish forever like his own dung. His youthful vigor lies with him in the dust."

"Evil," explained Zophar, "is like a sweet morsel in the mouth. You roll it around in your mouth as long as you can, but when it lands in your stomach it becomes sour like the venom of serpents. God makes you vomit it back up. In the same way, all the pleasures the godless man enjoys at the expense of others are given back, undigested. His prosperity will not endure, to the sorrow of his children, who have to make amends to the poor.

"The wicked man who gorges himself will experience God's burning anger like an iron weapon, a bronze-tipped arrow that pierces his back right to his liver. Terror and total darkness will come upon him. God's wrath, like a flood, will carry off his house. Such is the fate God allots the wicked, the heritage appointed for them by God."

Zophar was good at making sweeping statements which were truths in theory, but not the whole truth. Yes, God rewards the good and punishes the wicked, but in this life the delineation is often blurred. His implication, of course, was that Job was suffering because he was unrighteous. For all Zophar's flowery examples, that point was clear.

Job saw through Zophar's reasoning right away. He had known thoroughly unrighteous people who lived long lives, rich and powerful, with their children well established around them and their homes safe and free from fear: "Their bulls never fail to breed; their cows calve and do not miscarry. They send forth their children as a flock; their little ones dance about."

I thought about our precious sons and daughters, who loved to sing and dance. When Job played his flute and I banged the tambourine, how they would fly!

Yes, the wicked and the good both enjoy music. They both spend their years in prosperity and go down to the grave in peace. Yet the wicked have no desire to know God's ways. Who is God to them, that they should serve Him, or pray? God is the impartial pourer of His gifts on the godly and ungodly alike. The writing of the Ancients says that this is so, and experience bears it out as well.

Yet the lamp of the wicked is snuffed out. Calamity comes upon them. When scourge and pestilence come, we are all straws before the wind. We are all chaff swept away by a gale. When a cyclone hits the coast, we all suffer wind and rain alike. Were we spared flooding because we loved God? Not at all! Our rich soil washed away, mixing with the loam of our neighbor who cared not a whit for God.

One difference Job and I have noted: The wicked man cares little about the family he leaves behind when his allotted months come to an end. The man who loves God is concerned for the future of his loved ones. Job and I talked often about what would happen to me if he should die first. Our eldest son was well aware of his responsibility.

We cannot understand God's judgments. One man dies in full vigor, completely secure and at ease; another man dies in bitterness of soul, never having enjoyed anything good. Side by side they lie in the dust, and worms cover them both. However different we may be in life, we are alike in death. No matter how sweet the soil covering the grave, no matter how many the mourners in the funeral procession, the evil and the good are equally dead. Zophar's argument that Job suffered because he was wicked was nonsense.

Now Eliphaz had to add his two shekels worth. He could not imagine God's chastising a man for his piety. What would God gain by rebuking a righteous man? He accused Job of an endless number of sins, from slandering his brothers to mistreating widows and orphans. Perhaps that is the way wealthy land owners treated their people in Teman, but that was not Job's way.

"Is not God in the heights of heaven?" asked Eliphaz. "And see how lofty are the highest stars!" We looked up through the smoky haze at the twinkling lights. We knew that God was there, judging us through the darkness. Even thick clouds could not veil Him. He saw us as He went about in the vaulted heavens. Eliphaz accused Job of performing evil deeds in the assumption that God wouldn't notice. Of all men, Job was the most faithful in acknowledging God's mercy and judgment. Daily we had thanked Him for filling our house with good things. Daily we had offered sacrifices for our sins. Eliphaz was either a liar or totally unacquainted with Job's integrity. It was hard for me not to favor the former evaluation.

"Submit to God and be at peace with him," was Eliphaz's pious advice. If Job wanted restoration and prosperity, he had to accept God's teachings, repent and return. Repent for what? Job was not harboring any sin in his heart. Did Eliphaz want Job to invent some sins so he could earn God's favor?

An aged and venerable man, Eliphaz was due respect, but I could not honor a man who was so unjust, so vindictive. Job needed compassion, not advice. Yet Eliphaz, who was so emotional about his religious beliefs, was completely unemotional about Job.

Perhaps Eliphaz realized he had gone too far, I don't know. He offered Job a new perspective. Others would be more likely to profit from Job's goodness than himself. "When men are brought low and you say, 'Lift them up!' then God will save the downcast. He will deliver even one who is not innocent, who will be delivered though the cleanness of your hands." Whether or not Job benefited from his suffering, it would help others.

As the night deepened, I reflected on the fact that each of us is linked to others. We are all part of a vast web of humanity. On the horizontal plane no one's suffering is ever completely private. Cause and effect form an endless chain. On the vertical plane the consequences of evil are inherited from our ancestors, shared with our contemporaries, and bequeathed to the next generation. So it goes and so it has ever gone.

Chapter 18

The night, so black, suggested the darkness of Job's soul. Gradually the sky turned gray, then yellow streaked with rose. Like an alabaster pendant the morning star appeared.

Job spoke: "If only I knew where to find God; if only I could go to His dwelling! I would state my case before Him and fill my mouth with arguments. I would find out what He would answer me, and consider what He would say." Job knew he would get a fair hearing from God. But east, west, north, south, he could catch no glimpse of Him.

However, God had not lost sight of Job. "He knows the way that I take; when He has tested me, I will come forth as gold," he said emphatically. I looked up, surprised. Had Job's spiritual dawn come at last? What was this new tone of assurance in his voice? "My feet have closely followed his steps; I have kept to his way without turning aside. I have not departed from the commands of His lips; I have treasured the words of His mouth more than my daily bread."

And yet Job was still terrified by the Almighty. God carries out His decrees and does whatever He pleases. Sometimes His judgments are swift and harsh; sometimes He seemingly lets injustice go on without lifting a hand. Job reflected on all the evils of society that he had seen: thievery, oppression of the poor, exploitation of the homeless, even slavery. "The groans of the dying rise from the city, and the souls of the wounded cry for help. But God charges no one with wrongdoing."

What about personal evils? Murder, adultery, robbery — these, too, continue under the cover of darkness as if God couldn't see. Oh, yes, eventually those who prey on others die like the righteous, but only after enjoying their stolen goods. Like ears of corn, they are not lopped off until they have reached full maturity.

We who believe in a great and sovereign God can become convinced that for all God's inscrutability, His purposes are easily discernible in the daily round of life. But it is in living day by day that we repeatedly come up against experiences that deny this assumption. We cannot explain why one person is sick and another well, why one prospers and another fails, why calamities strike some and miss others. A child dies, a crop fails, and we do not know why. We must simply accept the fact that God knows what He is doing, and He will be glorified.

Job had proven his point that sometimes God does not punish evil, and sometimes He does not reward good. What he could not yet accept was the fact that God sometimes punishes good. This concept was against everything Job believed about God. His dilemma remained.

Bildad, of course, couldn't resist saying a few words on behalf of God. "Dominion and awe belong to Him; He establishes order in the heights of heaven." He considered Job arrogant indeed to think he could be righteous before God. If even the moon and the stars are not pure in God's eyes, how much less man, who is a maggot—a son of man, who is only a worm!

Well, we were all getting first-hand experience about maggots. I had but to squint my eyes and the whole dump looked as though it was moving. Yes, we had more than enough reminders that man is corrupt and full of decay. And worms? These lowly creatures burrowed through the earth all around us, as abased as we.

Job's dawn had been brief. A thick darkness again covered his face. But he would not be silenced. If all the words that flowed from his mouth had really been water, how refreshed we all would have been. Call me a disloyal wife, if you wish, but that's how I felt!

Chapter 19

I guess if a person who is sick nigh to death can still talk, and talk so much, that is something for which to be thankful. Job even had enough spirit left to be sarcastic. Bildad was a great encouragement, he was! He must have had help to display such great insight!

Job agreed that God is almighty. Minds of the present and the past can search out only the outskirts of His ways. Job reflected on the creation of the earth, how God spread out the northern skies over empty space, how He suspended the earth over nothing. "He wraps up the waters in his clouds, yet the clouds do not burst under their weight." I had often thought about that. "He marks out the horizon on the face of the waters for a boundary between light and darkness. The pillars of the heavens quake, aghast at his rebuke."

Then there was the sea, churned up by God's power. A legend persisted that a sea monster had lived in the deep. One day, after a terrible storm, parts of the beast were found floating onto the beach. No one had been foolish enough to take a boat out in the storm, so it was concluded that God had done the slicing Himself.

Job knew that God was all-powerful. In fact, he could teach Zophar, Bildad, and Eliphaz a few things about the power of God. He knew that God was everywhere. He believed that God was just. The question was: If God is just, why had He inflicted Job with such great suffering? Job would not deny his integrity. He would never let go of his righteousness; his conscience had not reproached him. Surely, he deserved a better fate than the wicked, whose good fortune, like his, was so temporary. Like the flimsy hut of a watchman in a vineyard, which a puff of the east wind can destroy, everything he owned was gone. There was no escaping God's judgments.

Then Job fell into a philosophical mood, sort of a mental interlude. He reminisced about his trip to Egypt when he visited the mines. I could not understand what had brought this on, but in his condition it's no wonder his mind wandered.

Where can wisdom be found, Job wanted to know. Not in the depths of the earth among the sapphires and nuggets of gold. Not on land or in the sea. Wisdom cannot be bought for any price. It is with God alone.

One time we had taken all the children on a trip to the sea. They were awed by so much water. "Does God know how much water there is?" they asked.

"Oh, yes," Job answered, "down to the last spoonful."

As so often happens, a storm came up very quickly, and we huddled together in our tent, looking out through the flap at the lightning. The little ones were frightened by the thunder, so we held them close. "Does God know where the storm will go?" they asked. Job assured them that God decided when it should storm, and where, to the final drop of rain and crack of thunder.

"God knows everything," he said. "If we wish to be wise, we will fear Him for all He knows."

Now that Job's memory was stirred, he thought about his former days, when God's watchful care had been like a lamp shining over his head. How he missed this intimate friendship with God! One by one he recounted all the good times until I cried out, "Stop! Why torture yourself? Why torture me? *I, me, my*, over and over again! Don't I count? Wasn't I there?"

But Job was not to be impeded from his downhill slide into self-pity and self-righteousness. All the detestation he was enduring from the hands of others now came to the fore. Oh, yes, he had been hurt, and he had not forgotten. I sat there in the dung, realizing for the first time Job's identification with the wealthy class. Whether or not he agreed with them, he was one of them and subject to the reprehension of those who had suffered at their hands.

The prestige that Job had enjoyed disappeared when he was struck with his infirmities. Young men, whose fathers Job would have disdained to put with his sheep dogs, now came out to the edge of Mazbalah and made fun of him. "Job, Job, covered with pus.

When you scratch your scabs, don't come near us!"
they sang over and over again. Gangs of young men
acting on a dare would approach us, trying to spit in
Job's face. We would drive them off, only to have
them reappear, braying their songs like wild donkeys,
completely unrestrained.

Job's suffering was three-fold, for the scorn he experienced from former admirers was accompanied by
terrible physical torment. The constant gnawing pain
made sleep impossible. His skin had turned black from
disease. Shreds of flesh hung down like wool sheared
from a sheep. His body was burning with fever. But
his decaying body was not nearly as painful as the
feeling churning in his stomach that God had rejected
him. "He throws me into the mud, and I am reduced to
dust and ashes," he cried.

He felt like a boat tossed about in a storm, abandoned, at the mercy of wind and sea. Where was God?
Why didn't He answer? Job had wept for those in trouble, but now that he was grieving, no help came. "I
have become a brother of jackals, a companion of
owls." Job's despondency was overwhelming his soul.
"My harp is tuned to mourning, and my flute to the
sound of wailing."

There was no joyful dancing now. Gone was the
piping of merry tunes, the jangle of the tambourine.
The only music was the quiet dripping of Job's tears.

My husband had been a righteous man: honest in
business, faithful in marriage, fair to his servants, gen-

erous to the needy, true to God, modest, hospitable. In a court of law he would be declared innocent of any wrongdoing. Job could give God an account of every step he had taken. He had nothing to hide.

None of Job's friends had found a way to refute Job, and yet they had condemned him. They sat in the ashes, with nothing to say. God did not speak, either.

Chapter 20

Job had a friend named Barakel, a Buzite of the family of Ram. The two men had grown up together, studying at the same school. When Job and I were married, Barakel attended, and brought with him an exquisitely woven rug as a wedding gift. Barakel's first-born son, Elihu, had always been a favorite of Job's because of his keen mind and ability to debate with his elders.

Job had a dream that Elihu would marry into our family. Had our daughters lived, I am sure Job and Barakel would have made the arrangements. Elihu would be a fine catch. Not only was he smart, but godly as well. His name, which means "whose God is he," was well chosen.

We were sitting on the dung hill, barely surviving the intense noonday sun, when who should cast his shadow over our stinking bodies but Elihu! He had been standing with a small crowd of curious onlookers earlier in the day, but now he stepped forth, drew his head dress back from his face, and revealed himself.

His beard was bushier now, his skin more weathered. If only I had a daughter to give him now!

Looking at the young man more intensely, I could see that he was scowling. Indeed, he was very angry — at Job and at his three friends. "I am young in years, and you are old," he acknowledged. "That is why I was fearful, not daring to tell you what I know. I thought, 'Age should speak; advanced years should teach wisdom.' But it is the spirit in a man, the breath of the Almighty, that gives him understanding. It is not only the old who are wise, not only the aged who understand what is right."

Well! These were brave words from one who had suffered so little. If he really was speaking from God's Spirit, he would have to prove himself. Job was surprised, but he waited to hear what words of enlightenment were going to pour forth from Elihu's youthful mouth.

Elihu boldly accused Eliphaz, Bildad, and Zophar of having inadequate answers to Job's questions. Not one of them had proven Job wrong. None of them had answered his arguments. He was tired of waiting and now felt compelled to have his say. "I am like bottled-up wine, like new wineskins ready to burst." (He looked it.) "I must speak and find relief; I must open my lips and reply. I will show partiality to no one, nor will I flatter any man; for if I were skilled in flattery, my Maker would soon take me away." (I didn't know about that. I could think of a lot of people skilled in flattery who were doing very nicely.)

Now Elihu turned to Job. "Listen to my words; pay attention to everything I say." This was rather bold direction from one not advanced in years, but Elihu claimed his words were coming from an upright heart. His lips were sincerely speaking what he knew. He was going to challenge Job to answer his assessment of Job's condition. Since both men were equal before God, having alike been taken from clay, Job should not be afraid.

Then Elihu got down to business, pointing out to Job where he was wrong. He had heard Job say that he was pure and without sin, yet God had found fault with him and considered him His enemy. "But I tell you, in this you are not right, for God is greater than man. Why do you complain to Him that He answers none of man's words?" he said in an accusatory tone.

In Elihu's opinion God does speak, even though man may not perceive it. Sometimes He uses a dream or a vision in the night. To turn us from wrongdoing and keep us from pride, God may speak in our ears with terrible warnings. "Or a man may be chastened on a bed of pain with constant distress in his bones," Elihu shot a hard look at Job, "so that his very being finds food repulsive and his soul loathes the choicest meal. His flesh wastes away to nothing, and his bones, once hidden, now stick out. "

This was an apt, if unkind, description. Job was half the size he had been before his affliction, and truly his arms and legs were like sticks. His skin hung down like the wattles of a chicken. He could not keep any food in his stomach. Even a cup of water caused him to retch.

But physical suffering was only part of his misery. As Elihu then pointed out, "His soul draws near to the pit, and his life to the messengers of death." If a man had a mediator, an angel, for example, to speak on his behalf, then the man's flesh would be renewed like a child's; it would be restored as in the days of his youth. The man would pray to God and find His favor. He would see God's face and shout for joy. Restored to his righteous state, the man would then go to his friends and tell them how he did not get what he deserved, even though he had sinned. "He redeemed my soul from going down to the pit, and I will live to enjoy the light."

Could this really happen? Could the wizened, emaciated man sitting cross-legged in our circle enjoy the freshness of a new childhood? My memory brought back the picture of Job when I first saw him walking down the road past our house. He was tall for his age, extremely handsome, with a stride that spoke of purpose. Here was a young man who was going places!

I arranged to be in the market place on the day he came with his brothers to do some trading. Just seeing him at the pottery stall made my heart jump like a spring locust. I was examining a water jar when he came over and spoke to me. To me! His voice was warm, but it was his eyes (when I dared to look up) that made me burn with longing. Full of feeling, those eyes, windows of a passionate house.

I knew, as every woman knows, that he found me attractive. I went home and told my father it was Job that I wanted to marry. He made the proper inquiries, found the family suitable, and made the necessary arrangements. For twelve months we waited, getting to know each other in chaperoned situations that allowed us little more physical contact than holding hands. But the fire was there. We kept it banked until our wedding night when our mutual love blazed with an ardor that must have humbled the stars.

Now Elihu was promising that we could go back? If that were true, what was the price? Job would have to acknowledge his suffering to be punishment for his sin. That was just what the other friends had said. That was something Job did not believe, for he had lived a righteous life.

Now Elihu was feeling quite bold. "Pay attention, Job, and listen to me; be silent, and I will speak." (This from a young man who had yet to trim his beard!) "If you have something to say, answer me; speak up, for I want you to be cleared. But if not, then listen to me; be silent, and I will teach you wisdom." We were all getting a lesson in audacity.

Elihu was not finished, not by any means. He turned to the three men in the circle and said, "Hear my words, you wise men; listen to me, you men of learning. For the ear tests words as the tongue tastes food. Let us discern for ourselves what is right; let us learn together what is good." Us? Learning together? With Elihu the teacher?

Chapter 21

How insensitive some religious people are! We bare our souls before them, seeking their comfort, and all they can do is mouth theological maxims that we have heard a dozen times before. The battered sufferer asks, "Why?" and receives nothing but old answers these prisoners of theory have worked out in their own minds.

Elihu could review Job's basic position that he was innocent, and disagree with it. He could reiterate, for our benefit, that God the Almighty repays a man for what he has done and brings upon him what his conduct deserves. He could remind us that God sees everything, and thus the rich and poor alike are judged fairly. Nobility enjoys no partiality with God.

Job had heard all this before from the other three men (I refuse to use the word *friends* anymore). Job still did not think he deserved such great punishment. In spite of Elihu's barbed accusations that Job was sinful, rebellious, scornfully clapping his hands and multi-

plying his words against God, Job maintained that he
would be cleared.

Well, Elihu thought so too, but there was a condition. "If men are bound in chains, held fast by cords of
affliction, God tells them what they have done — that
they have sinned arrogantly. He makes them listen to
correction and commands them to repent of their evil. If
they obey and serve Him, they will spend the rest of
their days in prosperity and their years in contentment."

Elihu saw God using sin as a teaching device to
strengthen one's character. Perhaps you hadn't been so
very bad, even a little on the good side, but suffering
would make you better. This was a new insight, but
the same old problem remained. Those who obey and
serve God do not always spend the rest of their days in
prosperity and contentment. Job *had* obeyed and
served God in the first place, and look what happened
to him! Surely God hadn't put him through so much
just for the sake of his character!

It was at this point that I noticed a sudden drop in
temperature. I looked up at the sky and saw black thun-
derclouds building up in the north. Shivering, I pulled
my cloak tightly around my body. Job, who had so little
protection from the cold, resettled himself closer to the
fire. Bildad, Eliphaz, and Zophar were warmly clothed
and seemed to take little notice of the invading chill.
Elihu, now pontificating at length, was so wrapped up in
his own importance he didn't need a coat.

Elihu chose this moment to give Job some advice.
"Be careful that no one entices you by riches," he

warned. "Do not let a large bribe turn you aside."
Would wealth help us in our present distress? I have
never been one to disparage money, but I could not see
how it could relieve Job's physical condition. All the
money in the world won't heal if God is not willing.

However, offers of financial help had been notice-
ably lacking so far. Even the three so-called friends
had been generous with words but woefully parsimonious with their money.

"Remember to extol God's work," Elihu advised.
Had we forgotten how great is God, beyond our understanding? The number of His years is past finding out.
With an incredible portend of the weather, Elihu talked
about the power of the Lord. "He draws up the drops
of water, which distill as rain to the streams; the clouds
pour down their moisture (I looked again at the black-
ening sky) and abundant showers fall on mankind.
Who can understand how He spreads out the clouds,
how He thunders from his pavilion?" As if God were
directing a play, there was a tumultuous roar in the
heavens. I covered my ears in pain.

Now even Elihu was aware of the changing
weather. "See how He scatters his lightning about
Him, bathing the depths of the sea. This is the way He
governs the nations and provides food in abundance.
He fills His hands with lightning and commands it to
strike its mark. His thunder announces the coming
storm; even the cattle make known its approach." I
thought of our cows bellowing back at the sky.

"Listen! Listen to the roar of His voice, to the rumbling that comes from His mouth. He unleashes His lightning beneath the whole heaven and sends it to the ends of the earth. After that comes the sound of His roar; He thunders with His majestic voice. When His voice resounds, He holds nothing back." Now I was really alarmed. The face of the whole earth was blacker than I had ever seen.

Elihu called us to stop and consider God's wonders. Did we know how God controls the clouds and makes His lightning flash? We did not. Did we know how the clouds hang poised, those wonders of Him who is perfect in knowledge? We did not know. Our minds were as dark as the sky. Were the sun suddenly to break through, we would be blinded with its brightness. How much less could we bear to look upon the Almighty, beyond our reach and exalted in power.

A bolt of lightning caused us all to jump. The wind was of such a driving force that we could barely keep our seats. On the ridge we had known the hot sirroco wind, but this was different. I looked around at the five faces wrapped with cloth in a futile attempt to escape the lashing gusts of sand and ashes that bruised our cheeks. The great sages were at last shaken, but Job looked peaceful, even expectant. He had been trying to storm the gates of heaven. Perhaps God was ready to answer!

Suddenly, Elihu stopped speaking. Preoccupied as we were with a strange, overwhelming fear, we hardly noticed.

Chapter 22

Has God ever spoken to *you?* Or did you ever *think* that God had spoken to you?

We know that God speaks to us through the writings of the Ancient Ones. That is the most reliable way to hear His words. Some people, like Eliphaz, believe that God can speak to us in dreams. Bildad listened to the scholarship of former generations. Elihu, who said that God spoke to him "from afar," agreed with Eliphaz about dreams and visions and added that God can speak to us through chastening on a bed of pain.

God can use our circumstances to answer questions that we ask Him, but have you ever heard God's voice? I mean, firsthand, the actual sound of words *at the moment that He is speaking them?* Few people have had this experience, and let me tell you, it is terrible and beautiful at the same time.

Out of the storm the Lord spoke to Job. Directly to *him.* Job's friends thought that God would never condescend Himself to speak to a man. He was too great to be bothered with such business. But they were wrong. God is personal, near at hand. He cares and He is willing to reveal His passion.

Job knew this. Oh, he had argued with God, as though God could be wrong, but in that very arguing he had testified that God was alive and listening. Would we argue with a god of stone? Would we expect a god of wood to answer back? Job had accused God of being silent, but he had never accused God of being dead.

Why hadn't God spoken sooner? Perhaps Job hadn't been ready to listen. If Elihu had done anything good, he had prepared Job's heart so that his ears were open to hear directly from God. His agitated soul was quiet at last.

Now it was God's turn to question. Out of the storm the Lord answered Job. He said, "Who is this that darkens my counsel with words of knowledge? Brace yourself like a man; I will question you, and you will answer Me."

Oh, yes, it was a powerful voice with an authority that caused us to shake with fear. And yet, it was a voice of infinite tenderness, pity, concern. Who but our God could exhibit such an ironhanded compassion?

At the command of God's voice to brace himself like a man, Job straightened his back. For the first time in many days, he changed his posture of dejection and looked up to hear God say, "Where were you when I laid the earth's foundation? Tell Me, if you understand. Who marked off its dimensions? Surely you know!"

Of course, Job wasn't on hand to watch God measure and construct the earth, although it must have been a joyous time. "The morning stars sang together and all the angels shouted for joy," God told us.

God reminded Job that he had no power at all. "Have you ever given orders to the morning, or shown the dawn its place, that it might take the earth by the edges and shake the wicked out of it?" I had to smile as I pictured our housekeepers shaking out our bed mats before rolling them up for the day.

"The earth takes shape like clay under a seal; its features stand out like those of a garment." Oh, yes, we knew what God was talking about. So many times Job had written on clay tablets and then stamped his seal. Baked in the sun, these tablets developed a hardness that defied disintegration. Did we not even now feel the sharp pieces of discarded writings that had been thrown in the trash heap?

We acknowledged that God had formed the earth without any help from us. Did we think, though, that because we had changed its contours or nurtured seeds, that we had been creators of anything?

I glanced at Job and knew he was sharing my thoughts. "Forgive us, Lord, for thinking there is any power in us," I prayed.

God had more questions. "Have you journeyed to the springs of the sea or walked in the recesses of the deep? Have the gates of death been shown to you? Have you seen the gates of the shadow of death?"

No, Lord, we know little about the sea, and nothing about the gates of death, except that we shall pass through them some day, as did our beloved children. I know they are in Your good hands, Lord. Will we see them again?

Now God spoke with a sarcasm that tore Job's heart. "What is the way to the abode of light? And where does darkness reside? Can you take them to their places? Do you know the paths to their dwellings? Surely you know, for you were already born! You have lived so many years!"

Job covered his gaunt face with his hands. "No, Lord," he whispered. "I have lived but a moment. My understanding is nothing."

How easily we can venerate our own age, I thought. By virtue of our longevity we think we become gods!

God was far from finished. "Have you entered the storehouses of the snow or seen the storehouses of the hail, which I reserve for times of trouble, for days of war and battle?"

Hail was uncommon in our area, but when it came it was always severe. One year the icy pellets were the size of small apples. As we huddled together while the house was bombarded, our second son asked if God was pitching hailstones out of a giant box. Children have a picturesque way of looking at things, do they not?

Did we know the source of lightning, or the east winds? Did we decide where the rain would fall? No, we had no control of such matters. "Does the rain have a father? Who fathers the drops of dew? From whose womb comes the ice?"

We sat in humiliation, staring down at the burned dung. We were totally helpless to do anything about the weather. God determined it all.

The wind continued to blow with great force, whipping our clothes around our bodies. After all the words that had poured out of our mouths, we had nothing to say. There were only the sounds of the wind, and God.

Chapter 23

I think there exists in each of us, deep down and hidden, the fear that there is some area of life which is beyond God's control. I have observed that it is usually some trivial matter which makes us doubt, like the day I chased goats out of the garden *three* times. We swat a fly and miss, or stub our toe, and cry out to God, "Can't You manage these vexations so that I am not tormented?"

God's reminders of His sovereignty were severe, but also loving. Again the questions boomed out above the storm, reminding us that His dominion extended over everything, whatever its seeming significance: "Do you know the laws of the heavens? Can you raise your voice to the clouds and cover yourself with a flood of water?"

The writings of the Ancient Ones told us of the great flood which covered the earth for forty days and forty nights. No one but God could have sent such a rain.

"Do you send the lightning bolts on their way? Do they report to you, 'Here we are'?"

I smiled. Right there, at such an awesome time, I laughed just a little at God's joke. I could just imagine a lightning bolt dropping by to tell us where it was going to strike!

"Who endowed the heart with wisdom or gave understanding to the mind?" (I hoped the three great sages were listening.) "Who has the wisdom to count the clouds? Who can tip over the water jars of the heavens when the dust becomes hard and the clods of earth stick together?"

What a poet God is! How I would love to tell my grandchildren about God's water jars. But there would never be little ones sitting on my lap and saying, "Tell me a story." Oh, I missed the children so much! God's dominion is not easy to acknowledge when it falls between the flies and the constellations.

God then described with a delighted wonder and love the creatures He had made. It had never occurred to me that God *enjoyed* His creation. I thought He formed everything and that was that. But when God talked about the lioness and the raven, whose young cry out to Him for food, there was a warmth in His voice, a paternalistic tone, that surprised me.

"Do you know when the mountain goats give birth?" He asked. "Do you watch when the doe bears her fawn?" We had often seen the little ones on the mountainside, but no wild animal would share a birthing with human eyes. As well acquainted as I was with labor pains, I had never thought of a doe having any. God remembered.

Then God asked about the wild donkey. It cannot be tamed to work for man but ranges the hills for pasture, even laughing at its subservient brothers responding to the whip and shout on the roads below! Wild donkeys are wily creatures and can live to be one hundred years old. Their meat is delicious, but what prowess is required in a hunter who wants to catch one! As for the wild ox, it cannot be relied on for heavy work. Foolish would be the farmer who would leave his threshing roller to an animal so unwilling to serve. Such freedom is God's gift. Job with all his power could not control it.

God even expressed His love for the ostrich, a bird which, in my estimation, is not very bright. She is a terrible mother, but, oh, can she run! A friend of ours tells the story of a day when he was riding across the desert, and an ostrich passed him!

The horse is a magnificent animal, strong and swift. "Do you make him leap like a locust, striking terror with his proud snorting?" God asked. "He paws fiercely, rejoicing in his strength, and charges into the fray. He laughs at fear, afraid of nothing; he does not shy away from the sword." God really loves the horse.

Job's humility had become humiliation at this point, but God wasn't finished. "Does the hawk take flight by your wisdom and spread his wings toward the

south? Does the eagle soar at your command and build
his nest on high?"

Many times we had sat on the ridge and watched
the great birds as they flew higher than we would ever
go. *What do we look like from up there,* we wondered.
Job supposed we would appear to be very small, just
the way people look to us when we see them in the
valley far below.

The eagle has a penetrating vision that can spot a
coney or a mouse hidden by their color from our
human eyes. An animal thus discovered is doomed.
With a mighty swoop the hapless creature is picked up
and carried off to feed the eaglets squawking in the
nest. How quickly they develop a thirst for blood! It is
awesome to think how this instinct to kill is passed on
from the parents to their young.

More amazing, I think, is how the instinct to kill is
passed on from human parents to their young. Wars
never end. Revenge is given as a justifiable reason to
destroy. Greed is not so easily justified but is often the
reason. Some people kill just because they love killing.
We had a group of soldiers stay overnight with us
once, on a trek to the north. One young man, barely
out of school I guessed, was permanently scarred by
the mutilation he had caused or seen on the battlefield.
His sleep was interrupted with terrible nightmares of
headless bodies. When he talked about anything, you
knew part of his mind was dwelling on blood and vis-
cera, spilled on the ground.

In the same group, however, was a soldier who positively delighted in swinging his sword to cut off a head or an arm. He could recount the goriest of battles and then fall asleep instantly, snoring so loudly the other soldiers moved their bedrolls far away. When he launched forth on one of his tales, I had the children quickly taken outside. Their propensity to do evil needed no prompting from a graphic story teller.

And now God's voice was close enough to penetrate the marrow of our bones. "Will the one who contends with the Almighty correct Him? Let him who accused God answer Him!"

It was as if a giant hand had grasped Job by the throat, cutting off all sound. Tears washed down his cheeks, but he could not speak.

Chapter 24

W e have all accused God of displeasing us in one
way or another, but let me tell you, hearing
God command His contender to face Him openly is
quite another matter! This was not God putting His
arm around Job's shoulder and speaking in a brotherly
fashion. This was God the omnipotent Father, very
stern and angry.

Job had sounded the same way the day three of our
sons criticized him for making them work in the fields.
"That is servants' work," they said, not looking nearly
as confident as they had when they agreed out behind
the house to take such an arrogant, unheard of position
of defiance.

Unlike our sons, Job was deeply repentant. "I am
unworthy—how can I reply to You? I put my hand
over my mouth. I spoke once, but I have no answer—
twice, but I will say no more."

Then the Lord spoke to Job out of the storm:
"Brace yourself like a man; I will question you, and

you shall answer Me." That sounded just like Job as he stood before his three trembling boys!

The Lord had more questions for Job. "Would you discredit My justice? Would you condemn Me to justify yourself? Do you have an arm like God's, and can your voice thunder like His?" Well, Job's voice could certainly thunder, but he was a whisper compared to God!

God threw out a challenge: "Then adorn yourself with glory and splendor, and clothe yourself in honor and majesty. Unleash the fury of your wrath, look at every proud man and bring him low, look at every proud man and humble him, crush the wicked where they stand."

Ah, when Job was dressed in his finest robes, his bracelets and rings catching the rays of the sun, he was a sight to behold! The servants would oil his skin and his hair so that they shone too. I loved looking at him and could have eaten him with my eyes. I loved the way he smelled, too. The odor of spikenard would fill the house.

I confess that some of my thoughts were far from matters of state or religion when Job adorned himself. Oh, yes, I worshiped God at His holy altar. I truly did. But there was a part of me, a tiny but torrid part, that anticipated the intimacy of us in each other's arms. I would almost faint from the joy of it.

But here was God showing how very insignificant Job's splendor was compared to His. No earthly adornment could possibly rival the honor and majesty with which God dressed Himself. Only God could look at every proud man and humble him. Only God could bury the proud and the wicked in the dust together. Only He could shroud their faces in the grave.

If Job had any vestige of pride left because he was a man, God went on to extol the qualities of a hippopotamus! "What strength he has in his loins, what power in the muscles of his belly! His tail sways like a cedar; the sinews of his thighs are close-knit. His bones are tubes of bronze, his limbs like rods of iron."

Job and I took a trip to Egypt many years ago, and we saw a hippopotamus in the great river. He was lying under the lotus plants, hidden among the reeds in the shadow of a grove of poplars. The other birds and animals did not seem to mind him at all, but our host said he was fierce by nature and very difficult to catch. We had no intention to try.

It was this homely, cumbersome creature that God was calling first among the works of God. A hippopotamus!

Then God praised the crocodile, another animal I would hardly rank first for either good looks or usefulness. We readily acknowledged that we could not pull him to shore with a fishhook or tie down his tongue with a rope. We could not put a cord through his nose or pierce his jaw with a hook.

"Can you make a pet of him like a bird or put him on a leash for your girls?" God asked. Like all families, our children had their share of pets. Over the years the boys had eagles and hawks which they flew from cords attached to the birds' legs. I remember a goose which belonged to our youngest daughter. The silly thing followed her everywhere, in and out of the house, and proved a real trial to the servants who were constantly cleaning up her droppings. When the goose got so large it was dangerous, we had to send it, amidst loud wailings, to a farm on the other side of the city. There was no possibility that it could ever appear on our dinner table!

No, a crocodile would never be a pet. Nor would anyone want to buy one at the market. What use would he be if you could trap him? Any man who battles a crocodile comes away with one less arm or leg, if he comes away at all.

If we are overpowered by a mere crocodile, how can we stand up against God? Who has a claim against God that He must pay? Everything in heaven belongs to Him. He is omnipotent, the Creator and Sustainer of all life.

It was the most solemn of moments. We sat in the dung, each reflecting on our personal manifestations of pride. We had been children, babbling with an arrogance based on false wisdom. God was calling us to the maturity of silent contemplation.

Chapter 25

S wirling winds blew the surrounding debris into drifts that covered our crossed legs. Ashes and soot stuck in our ears and up our noses. We had to flail our arms to keep the miserable stuff out of our eyes. Although there was no rain, the darkness enshrouded us like a cloak. It was only by the sound of our bodies fighting off the flying bits of rubble that each of us knew we were not alone.

Sometime during the storm Elihu left. His departure was as mysterious as his arrival. Whether he felt that he had accomplished his purpose, or was frightened, we never knew. Perhaps he was tired of hearing about crocodiles! Now that I knew Elihu better I found him to be an insensitive man. He described himself as "one perfect in knowledge," a rather risky evaluation for anyone to have, if you ask me. He would have been a difficult son-in-law, I decided, and a difficult husband. What woman wants to be married to a man who knows everything?

Gradually the winds calmed. Likewise, Job's inner
turmoil settled and he replied to the Lord: "I know that
You can do all things; no plan of Yours can be
thwarted. You asked, 'Who is this that obscures My
counsel without knowledge?' Surely You spoke of
things I did not understand, things too wonderful for
me to know."

Will not a confession like that stand for all time?
All our inner storms would abate if we could say to
God, "I know that You can do all things; no plan of
Yours can be thwarted." Here are God's omnipotence
and His righteousness, not as segments of His divine
nature which can come and go, but as a circle, existing
as a continuum that has no beginning and no end.

I had loved Job for his body which was beautifully
proportioned, seemingly ageless. He emitted a virility,
an energy that attracted men and women alike. The
thirst for every drop of life that God could give was as
insatiable as it had been when he was a youth. Now he
was physically repulsive, emaciated, covered with oozing sores.

I had loved Job for his mind, his desire to know
everything. Always thinking about the world and what
was in it. So quick witted, how he could make me
laugh! He would administer our huge estate with ap-
parent ease, bartering with a shrewd eye, settling labor
disputes, deciding on flocks and crops, and then come
home with a bunch of anemones just for me.

Job's mind had been surprisingly alert in debate. I was amazed at his perception. He had taken no nourishment, been in constant pain, and yet his mind remained clear. Of course, he did not laugh, nor did I, and I certainly did not expect anemones, but could he not have looked at me and smiled a little? Could he not have reached out his hand — but no, I would have recoiled, wouldn't I? Job knew that. Oh, Job, forgive me for such obvious rejection!

I had loved Job for his — shall I call it — godliness. He loved and served the Lord, sacrificing faithfully on the altar, keeping the Lord's teachings. Of all the men in our city, no one equalled Job in concern for his family. Visitors in our home always thought it incredible that Job had only one wife, when he could have afforded so many more!

The morning star was shining in a sky slowly changing from black to deep blue. Job spoke to God again: "You said, 'Listen now, and I will speak; I will question you, and you shall answer Me.' My ears had heard of You but now my eyes have seen You. Therefore I despise myself and repent in dust and ashes."

Dust and ashes. That is a significant symbol among our people. To portray your worthlessness and debasement, pour ashes over your head, smear them over your body, permeate the threads of your robe until it is gray. Job had talked of dust and ashes before, but this time he *was* dust and ashes. This time he gladly accepted being reduced to less than nothing. Now he knew himself and now he knew God, for he had *seen* God.

I have observed that there are different ways to know God. Some who had shared our bread and wine had known Him as a subject to be discussed. They had much information and quoted extensively from the writings of the Ancient Ones. All their knowing was in their minds, and when Job asked them if the knowing had changed their lives, they would answer, "When we have learned everything, that will make a difference."

Some people only know God as He is reflected in other people. He is for them a secondhand experience. They hear their friends talk about how God supplies every need, and they believe it, but they have never trusted God completely themselves. I am reminded of the spice merchant who visited us on his way to the Great Sea. He knew of the one true God and believed in Him. He trusted Him for protection against thieves, but he traveled with an armed guard just far enough behind as to be out of sight.

Now Job had seen God. He had had a personal encounter with Him. God had become everything to him, and he had become less than nothing before God. Job knew the problem was not God, but himself. With that finding came an incomparable peace. Job had lost everything, but he had found his fellowship with God, and that was sufficient.

As the dawn spread over the eastern sky, so a new love for Job filled my heart. As God spoke to Job, so had He spoken to me, for what had I valued in a husband? Strong bones and straight teeth? The ability to make money? A lust for all that made me a woman? Faithful keeping of the law? What were they compared to a man who knew God! The body perishes, wealth is transitory, passion cools, but finding God is eternal and, indeed, the bedrock of all that comprises flesh and spirit.

Job had seen God, and so had I.

Chapter 26

The crisis was over. Job was at peace. He was still afflicted with painful sores from the soles of his feet to the top of his head. Pus oozed out, pasting his ragged dress to his skin. Physically nothing had changed, but there was hope shining out of his puffed eyes, a certain settling of his shoulders that was fortitude rather than resignation.

We were uncertain what we should do. As the sky brightened we stretched and changed position. The three friends gave no indication that they were going home, although it seemed they had no more advice to give.

We were greatly startled when the Lord spoke again, directly to Eliphaz, the mystic. "I am angry with you and your two friends, because you have not spoken of Me what is right, as My servant Job has." The blame was for speaking wrongly about the Lord, not about Job, I noted with interest. "So now take seven bulls and seven rams and go to My servant Job and sacrifice a burnt offering for yourselves. My servant Job will pray for you, and I will accept his prayer and not deal with you according to your folly. You have not spoken of Me what is right, as My servant Job has."

"My servant Job will pray for you!" God, who knows our hearts, was sure of Job, but I, human that I am, had a vestige of uncertainty. Job was uncommonly righteous, I knew that, but to pray for Eliphaz, Bildad, and Zophar was asking a lot. They had given him nothing but recrimination, offering not a shred of comfort. I would have argued with God about that expectation.

The three men left the dung heap and returned late in the afternoon to carry Job up on the ridge where they had prepared the altar of sacrifice. It was the first time that anyone had touched Job since he was afflicted, and the experience was unsettling to them all. Job was light enough to be born by one man, but, since no one wanted that much bodily contact, the three friends awkwardly shared the load. The look on their faces was of absolute revulsion.

I trailed along behind, so grateful to be out of Mazbalah. I was going to bathe, and bathe again, scrubbing away the pollution that had permeated every pore in my body. I would wash my hair until pure water flowed into the bowl. Then I would put on a clean dress, its beauty and quality not mattering in the slightest. I had been a dung heap myself, and it made me sick. I was consumed with a passion to wash.

We arrived on the ridge, where the seven rams and seven bulls were stomping about in their hastily erected pens. Large stones had been arranged to form a platform waist high. Urns of water, long knives, and basins for catching the blood were at the side. Smoke from a pot of coals rose straight up in the late afternoon air.

Job was gently lowered to the ground. I sat beside him, strangely stirred at the prospect of a burnt offering. I had not realized how much I missed worshiping God in this way. I, too, had sins which needed to be atoned for. I prayed that God would not deal with me as *I* deserved.

Sacrificing a burnt offering is a bloody business, as each animal is slaughtered and burned. Fourteen beasts take many hours to consume and leave behind a small mountain of bones. To one unfamiliar with the practice, animal sacrifice can be very distasteful. For those of us who belong to Jehovah, it is something we first see as suckling babies and is as natural as threshing wheat. We see beauty in the carnage, because we see God as the One who forgives our sins.

Job watched, and he prayed. The Lord accepted Job's prayer. We know that he did, because Job experienced a deep reassurance and peace. With this came the knowledge that he was once again accepted by God. Only a man accepted by God, and righteous in His sight, could mediate for his fellow men. Job had been vindicated.

After begging forgiveness, and exchanging warm embraces (the three friends actually hugged Job), the men parted company. Job and I were left alone on the

ridge. Fortunately the night was warm, so we simply
lay down on the ground and fell asleep in each other's
arms. My relief at the positive turn of events in our
lives overcame my disgust at Job's physical condition.
But I was not one to say that the body doesn't matter.
Surely we have to deal with the part of a person that
we see.

Since Job was far more exhausted than I, he slept
far into the morning. I awakened when the sun's rays
first hit my eyes. I propped myself up on one arm and
looked at him. Something was different, and at first I
couldn't define just what it was. Either my rekindled
love had drawn a veil over my eyes or Job had
changed.

The huge sores seemed to be growing smaller. His
skin was smooth and, though he was still very thin,
there was a more natural color. Whatever had happened, I was overcome with thankfulness that Job was
still alive. Men with lesser afflictions have succumbed,
but Job had not given up.

The tiny dwelling that we had left was still standing.
I found a water jar and went off to the well. By some
miracle there were lentils in a storage basket. Another
jar held olives. I remembered them as being empty, but
perhaps I was confused in the midst of so many trau-
matic events. I certainly wasn't getting senile!

By the time Job awoke I had porridge cooking, and
I was able to arrange the semblance of a meal, setting
it on a cloth spread on the ground. An arrangement of

flowers added a festive touch. When Job "followed his nose," as he put it, into the house, he was more delighted than if I had prepared a seven-course feast. He was ravenous but insisted that we first bow our heads in thanks to God. Then he picked up his bowl of lentils and drank with loud slurps, remarking over and over again at the remarkable quality of the porridge, its perfect consistency, its exquisite seasoning. I laughed and refilled his bowl. Was I going to tell him there *was* no seasoning, that the consistency was simply the result of the proportions of water and beans that I had on hand? Of course not!

Many olives later, Job's shrunken stomach was full. He lay back on his mat and groaned with pleasure, his eyes twinkling with expectation. "Shouldn't we wash first?" I asked.

"We can make love, and then wash, and make love again," he answered. With joy I crept into his arms. There was another appetite to be satisfied, and I was delighted to fill that one too!

Chapter 27

J ob went with me to the well. "What will people think?" I asked. No man goes to a well.

"Let them think what they wish," Job replied. "I am a new man!"

And he was. The sores had disappeared. His new skin was taut as a tent rope. There was crimson in his cheeks, a spring to his step. He almost danced along with his water jug, which really set the town gossips to talking!

Oh, how we washed. We poured water over each other and scrubbed each other's backs. We scoured between each toe and behind each ear. The soap suds looked like snow about our feet. When we were clean we rubbed our bodies with olive oil perfumed with myrrh and cassia. The scent was intoxicating. It filled the house and made us drunk with passion.

This time I slept while Job arose and went into town. His intention was to recultivate his business associations, to use his well-established reputation as collateral for obtaining a loan. He needed workers to plant crops, tend animals, restore the vineyards. His vast acreage could be productive again if he had help.

The response was amazing. People who had ostracized us now couldn't wait to lend us money. An excellent manager was found to hire workers. Soon the hills and valleys were alive with activity. Like ants in a pile of sand, the planters came, sowing seed, setting out young trees and vines. Herds of sheep and goats appeared. Brick layers and plasterers came to restore our buildings.

It was as if God was smiling on our endeavors. The weather was ideal, with sun and rain at just the proper times. The town folk commented that they had never seen such perfect weather. When the final harvest was brought in, Job announced that our wealth was twice as large as before!

When the news of our prosperity reached Job's brothers and sisters, they came to see for themselves. I regarded their visit with a cynical attitude, I admit, for where had they been during our time of distress? There had not been a word from any of them. They were not poor themselves, but they had offered us no help, not a grain of wheat nor a drop of oil. *Now* they were filling up our newly decorated rooms, gushing with comfort and consolation.

Job knew my feelings and urged me to be generous. Did it matter to us what was their motivation? God had blessed us abundantly, and we could share ten times over. I tried to be pleasant, but when they came forth with silver coins and gold rings I left to supervise the cooking. One *kesitah* would have made all the difference after our tragedy, not to mention the assurance that someone cared for us in our suffering.

It seemed that everyone who had ever known us came for a meal. The grinding wheel never stopped. The cooks were busy day and night keeping the pots full of savory stews. Slaughtering went on continually, and yet there was no shortage of animals. We could not use up all that the Lord had given us. I was stricken with guilt about my parsimonious attitude and offered special sacrifices on our altar.

Conceiving had never been a problem for me, so neither Job nor I was surprised that I was pregnant. My body was still strong, making an easy delivery possible. The child was a girl whom we named Jemimah, "a dove," because of her gentle, affectionate disposition. She was, indeed, easy to care for. Another girl followed, Keziah, named after the cassia plant whose fragrance always delighted us.

Of course we wanted sons, and God granted us seven. Handsome boys they were, strong and healthy, quick to learn. Finally, just when I thought my childbearing days were over, there came Keren-Happuch, which means "eye paint." It was a name associated with beauty, and quite fitting, for Keren was as beautiful as her sisters. Nowhere in all the land were there found women as beautiful as Job's daughters. Everyone said so.

The animals continued to multiply. When Job took inventory he counted fourteen thousand sheep, six thousand camels, a thousand yoke of oxen, and a thousand donkeys. He showed me the figures and waited for my reaction. *What was he expecting,* I wondered. I looked closely at the tablets. I had little experience with numbers and could make nothing of all those thousands.

Job settled back on his mat and smiled. "While cleaning out the barn this morning, our foreman found the tablets made by our accountant just before . . . just before we lost everything." His voice faltered ever so slightly. "In every case, our animals have exactly doubled in number. Doubled! What does that tell you?"

"That God has blessed us twice over!" I answered promptly.

"Exactly! God has given back everything that was taken, and more. The Lord gave and the Lord has taken away. The Lord has given again. May the name of the Lord be praised!" In grateful adoration we bowed our heads and thanked God.

That night, long after the children were asleep, we lay on our mats, recounting our blessings. The doubling of our animals was truly astounding, but then I was struck so forcibly by another statistic that I sat bolt upright. "Job!" I exclaimed. "Think about the children!"

"I do, all the time," he responded.

"I mean, think about the *number* of the children. We have ten!"

Job already knew how many children we had and was increasingly puzzled, so I explained. "If the number of animals we lost was doubled, why didn't God double the number of children in the same way?"

"Because they are not really lost!" he exclaimed, seeing my point. "Someday we shall see them all with our own eyes. Oh, how I yearn for that day!"

"As do I. My heart is greatly comforted to know that our children are safe and well, waiting for us."

I lay down again, filled with an overwhelming joy. For those who worship the true God, death is *not* the end. Parents and children will be reunited, to live forever with God. What a glorious truth! I lay in the warmth of Job's arms, and slept.

Chapter 28

A weakening of the flesh after a disease as severe as Job's would have been normal, but in his case strength and vigor returned in greater measure than before. There seemed no end to his energy as he visited every corner of our estate, inspecting the crops and animals, checking the fences and watch towers, seeing to the servants' needs.

The oversight of such a large number of workers was formidable. Then there was the buying and selling, the negotiations with travelers from every part of the earth. Added to these tasks was Job's position as a counselor at the city gates. People who could not meet him there came to the house, so the kitchen was busy all day, supplying refreshments. No visitor to our home ever went away without a full stomach and clean feet.

Ten children also kept Job busy, as he taught them about God, not in long lectures, but in hikes up the mountain or across the fields. It was not Job's intention that his children take their wealth for granted, so he expected them to learn and to work. The girls especially flourished under his care, since it was not normal in our culture for them to receive such attention.

When his daughters came of age, Job arranged for each of them to receive an inheritance so that they would never have to leave the family group. None of our girls would have to depend upon a husband who might consider her as just another piece of property to be taken far away.

As before, the brothers and sisters enjoyed a deep love for one another. As the years passed, they took over more and more of the management of our estate, although Job was not one to lie about indulging himself in food and drink. He was always on the move, seeking new ways to use what God had given him.

We were the typical grandparents when our eldest son had his first child. Then were the typical great grandparents when that son had his first child. Indeed, we were still proud and doting as great-great-grandparents. Our family was an entire community unto itself, numbering almost one thousand. And the Lord continued to make Job prosperous, providing food and shelter for all.

The oldest man in the city was Shemai, reported to be almost one hundred. His grandchildren would carry him out of the house and set him against the wall in the sun, where he would sit all day absorbing the warm rays. The street children would come up and look at Shemai, as if he were a curiosity like the two-headed calf that had been born on our farm during a terrible storm.

After Shemai died, there was no one to take over his role as city spectacle. On Job's one hundredth birthday he was out in the wheat fields, helping the threshers harvest a crop before the rains set in. On Job's two hundredth birthday he was dictating a new city code to his scribes. His mind remained clear, always curious about the wonders of God's creation, always probing for answers to life's mysteries.

Every morning without fail Job would sacrifice burnt offerings to God. He was our priest, offering atonement for our sins. God had commanded Job to brace himself like a man, and he did, trusting in God's power, secure in God's love. His beard changed from gray to white, his skin became wrinkled as a dried fig, but his vigor remained. The man bowing before the altar was as keen as a youth of twenty.

Old age is a terrible time for those filled with enmity toward God. Bitterness and hatred make miserable days. Death is a blessing, if only because it ends the pain that won't be healed any other way.

For Job, old age was a time of increasing joy as he was drawn closer and closer to God, more aware of His character, more awed by His love, more sure of a life beyond the grave. "I know that my Redeemer lives," he would say to me, not usually during his times of meditation, but rather when the almond trees blossomed or the ewes were birthing. One day it was prompted by an intensely brilliant rainbow. The next, by an ostrich egg in the hot sand.

He carried me along, Job did, almost willing me to
accompany him through his final days. I was tired and
ready to die, but Job's arm was there to support me on
a walk along the ridge. He himself rubbed my aching
legs with warm oil sweetened with myrrh. He guided
me along the path, describing tiny flowers that my
dimmed eyes could no longer see. I, in turn, had the
better hearing to discern a bird singing, the steps of
servants about the house.

Such a pair we were! Each helping the other, two
halves making a whole. Our daily worship now took
place at home, with Job offering the sacrifice in the
company of those who lived within our house. Job expressed again and again the yearning of his heart to see
God, not in his heart now, where God had graciously
and wondrously revealed Himself, but face to face in
the life that continues after the grave.

One night after the servants had tucked us in bed
(we become little children again!), I lay in Job's arms,
grateful for the warmth of the woolen blankets shield-
ing us from the chill that settled over everything when
the sun went down. Job's wizened body had long since
lost its heat, and my old bones were always cold.

His usual snoring had not yet begun, so I knew he
was awake. "What are you thinking about?" I asked.

"I was thinking about that time in Mazbalah. Do
you remember?"

"Remember! I have not forgotten a single detail!
The smoldering ashes, the stench, the broken pottery.

You with your body covered with oozing sores. It is all in my memory. That part of my mind hasn't aged."

"Nor mine. I can see the dump with Eliphaz and Zophar and Bildad and Elihu sitting there, expounding their great philosophies."

"And me. Can you see me?"

"Ah, yes, dearest wife, I can see you, smudged with soot."

"I wasn't much comfort. Do you remember what I said?"

"I've forgotten."

"You are a sweet liar. I told you to curse God and die. But you didn't. 'Shall we accept good from God, and not trouble?' you asked. Of course, we could not. We have had to accept both."

"Looking back, there has been so little trouble, and so much good. If we could only see around the corners of life, how easy it would be!"

"But then there would be no exercise in trust. We would miss knowing about God's faithfulness. His character would be incomplete. You taught me that yourself."

Job stroked my hair. "Marriage is teaching each other, isn't it?"

"A good marriage is learning together. Ours has been a very good marriage, don't you think?"

"Yes, a very good marriage." He was drifting off to sleep. "Good night, dear wife. I shall see you soon." He was snoring even as I kissed his wrinkled cheek.

Chapter 29

J ob died during the night. No gasping for breath. No clutching his chest. He simply slipped away to see God.

When I awoke I sensed instantly that he was dead. I have buried many people in my life, and I know the rigidness, the cool feeling of the skin.

I called to the servants, who came at once. With quiet efficiency Job's body was wrapped in linen cloths and placed on a bier. By noon family and friends had assembled in great numbers. I could not believe so many people had come! There was much sobbing and wailing as we slowly walked to the family tomb. Two of my grandsons offered me their arms and literally carried me all the way.

The priest spoke words written by the Ancient Ones. Then the body was placed in the tomb, and the stone rolled in front of the door. It slipped down the track and settled into place with a sharp thud, forever separating the dead from the living.

We walked back to the house, where friends had left food of every description. There was eating until the sun went down. My favorite servant led me gently into the house and put me to bed. For the first time in many years—was it hundreds?—I slept alone.

So here I sit, on a spring morning, looking at the purple iris and thinking about Job. "I shall see you soon," he had promised. Yes, my beloved, you shall. We were not meant to be alone, you and I.

We had a good life together. What was it Job had said? "My path was drenched with cream and the rock poured out for me streams of olive oil." God was watching over us, like a lamp shining upon our heads. But He was no less present in our despair. In the smoldering dung, God had not abandoned us.

"I know you have forgiven me, Lord, for telling Job to curse You and then die. There is no need to ask You again, but it is on my heart. Please don't mind the ramblings of an old woman."

I can hardly keep my eyes open. Ah, well, at my age, a little drowsiness is forgivable. The warm sun feels so good on my bones; it draws away the ache. My great-granddaughter sits quietly beside me, should I need an extra robe. She is a lovely child, but I cannot remember her name. So many children! So many names! My womb has sweet memories, even if my mind has forgotten.

Yes, a nap will feel good. I will close my eyes for a little while. When I block out the mountains and the ridge, I can see Job, standing strong and tall, his arms outstretched to welcome me. Did I enjoy my walk to see the lambs? Were the children well behaved? Oh, yes, dear Job, it was a perfect day, but I am so glad to be home with you at last!

ABOUT
THE AUTHOR

Author, teacher, and well-known speaker, Jean Shaw brings a wealth of experience and a genuine Christian joy to her writing. She is a graduate of Simmons College in Boston and earned her teaching certificate from the University of Pittsburgh. In addition, she holds a Master of Science degree in Home Economics (Marriage and Family Living) from Northern Illinois University and a Master of Arts degree in Biblical Studies from Covenant Theological Seminary.

Mrs. Shaw is a frequent speaker at various women's groups. She also finds time to serve on the Christian Education Committee of her church as well as to edit the church newsletter.

Jean has written five books (all published by Zondervan) and many journal articles. She enjoys gardening, reading, and travel and lives with her husband, Gordon D. Shaw, in Ballwin, Missouri. The Shaws are the parents of four children and the grandparents of seven.

The typeface for the text of this book is *Times Roman*. In 1930, typographer Stanley Morison joined the staff of *The Times* (London) to supervise design of a typeface for the reformatting of this renowned English daily. Morison had overseen type-library reforms at Cambridge University Press in 1925, but this new task would prove a formidable challenge despite a decade of experience in paleography, calligraphy, and typography. *Times New Roman* was credited as coming from Morison's original pencil renderings in the first years of the 1930s, but the typeface went through numerous changes under the scrutiny of a critical committee of dissatisfied *Times* staffers and editors. The resulting typeface, *Times Roman*, has been called the most used, most successful typeface of this century. The design is of enduring value to English and American printers and publishers, who choose the typeface for its readability and economy when run on today's high-speed presses.

Substantive Editing:
Michael Hyatt

Copy Editing:
Alice Ewing

Cover Design:
Steve Diggs & Friends
Nashville, Tennessee

Page Composition:
Xerox Ventura Publisher
Printware 720 IQ Laser Printer

Printing and Binding:
Maple-Vail Book Manufacturing Group,
York, Pennsylvania

Cover Printing:
Weber Graphics
Chicago, Illinois